Riano D. McFarland is a professional singer, songwriter, author, and entertainer, residing in Las Vegas, Nevada. He began writing poetry and short stories as a teenager in Mt. Juliet, Tennessee.

After enlisting in the United States Air Force in 1983, he was assigned to Neu Ulm, Germany. Being immersed in Europe's rich history and surrounded by some of the world's most iconic landscapes and architecture, his interest in creative writing was further fueled.

His flair for capturing the essence of his surroundings in words formed the building blocks of his writing style and allows readers to see through his eyes.

This book is dedicated to all "no-kill" animal shelters and their dedicated staff, tirelessly preserving the lives of rescued pets while helping to place them in new homes with loving families. You have my undying gratitude.

Riano D. McFarland

ODIN

AUSTIN MACAULEY PUBLISHERS™

LONDON · CAMBRIDGE · NEW YORK · SHARJAH

Ordering Information:
Quantity sales: special discounts are available on quantity purchases by corporations, associations, and others. For details, contact the publisher at the address below.

Publisher's Cataloging-in-Publication data
McFarland, Riano D.
ODIN

ISBN 9781643788890 (Paperback)
ISBN 9781643788906 (Hardback)
ISBN 9781645365518 (ePub e-book)

Library of Congress Control Number: 2019916882

The main category of the book — FICTION / Thrillers / Suspense

www.austinmacauley.com/us

First Published (2019)
Austin Macauley Publishers LLC
40 Wall Street, 28th Floor
New York, NY 10005
USA

mail-usa@austinmacauley.com
+1 (646) 5125767

Chapter One

Katherine was no marathon runner... not by a long shot, but today was one of her best morning jogs ever. She was nearly a full minute ahead of her previous record as she approached her final checkpoint, the rusty old Gatwick Bridge that crossed over Willis Creek. Beyond the bridge, Willis Creek widened dramatically, flowing into the river less than a mile from her house.

The morning fog was just starting to lift as she passed beneath the rickety metal structure that had been there since the late 1930's. Eyeing the rusted pillars skeptically, as she did every morning, she wondered when the County would finally condemn the bridge and replace it with a more modern structure.

As she dug in and concentrated on the home stretch, she was distracted by a loud splash in the river to her left. Looking back over her shoulder, she noticed something floating in the ice-cold water. Her initial feeling was outrage at the thought of locals using the river to dispose of their waste, without even the slightest consideration for the environment.

Before her mind could delve deeper into her internal rant, she heard something odd over the sound of the rushing river. It sounded like the high-pitched chirping of baby birds... not something you'd typically hear in February, with a foot of snow still blanketing the ground.

It took a moment for her to realize, the sound was coming from the sack floating past her in the river! They were the desperate cries of puppies, fighting for their lives inside a sinking burlap bag.

Katherine's jog became a run, and then a full-on sprint as she fought to close the distance between herself and the partially submerged bag. Racing to beat the river's pace to the boat dock behind her house, she knew it would be the last possible point of rescue. This had suddenly become a race she would not allow herself to lose!

Her lungs were burning as she reached the dock... her footsteps sounding loudly as she ran across the wooden planks.

Where was it? There were no longer audible cries echoing in the wooded bend. Had she missed it? By now the bag may have already been swept past the dock into the widening river beyond. Her heart sank at the thought, as she frantically scanned the surface of the river through tear-filled eyes. There! Just out of reach, the fully submerged bag was passing the end of the dock just below the surface. She was too late.

Screaming "NO, NO, NO!" at the top of her lungs, Katherine jumped!

Despite the shocking cold of the icy river, she swam out into the rushing water until she was able to grasp the end of the frayed rope trailing along behind the sinking bag. Pulling it out of the freezing water, she rolled onto her back and placed the bag on her abdomen, allowing the current to guide her toward the riverbank.

As she reached the shallows and her feet dug into the gravelly sand, she ran out of the water and didn't stop until she reached the back door of her house. Quickly entering the keyless entry code, she flung the door open, rushing to the warmth of the fireplace, desperately tugging at the rope tied tightly at the top of the bag. Ripping it open, she carefully placed seven tiny motionless bodies on the hearth, hoping and praying for any signs of life.

Briskly rubbing all of them in turn, she tried to get their circulation flowing again. They were all so very cold, and her sadness and frustration only mounted as their tiny lifeless bodies began to stiffen.

Suddenly, one of them coughed! It was barely audible, but in the otherwise deafening silence, it may just as well have been a klaxon.

The tiniest of them began to move. He was fighting for his life, surrounded by the corpses of his siblings.

Katherine now concentrated her efforts on saving this little runt. Ripping a piece from the BODINE FEED SUPPLY bag, she wrapped her little fighter in it, holding him tightly against her chest, allowing her body heat to warm him. After a while, he began to whimper softly. Within minutes, those whimpers had become squeaks, and he began nudging against her breast, fighting his way back to life.

Holding his little coal-black body close to her with one hand, Katherine heated milk in a saucepan while she rifled through the kitchen cabinets and drawers, looking for something she could use to feed it to him.

Finally, she found a tiny tincture tube dropper. Pouring warm milk into a coffee cup, she sat at the kitchen table and filled the dropper with it. The little pup took to it right away, drinking dropper after dropper until the cup was empty, and his little belly was full.

While he slept cradled in her arms, Katherine collected the bodies of all the other pups from the hearth, wrapped them together in a soft towel, and placed them in a large shoebox. She found a small blanket to replace the piece of the bag the sole survivor had been wrapped in earlier. As she picked it up, she noticed the letters imprinted on the fragment were O-D-I-N.

"Odin," she whispered out loud. For a moment, the pup opened his little blue eyes and seemed to look up at her before falling back to sleep. Judging by his deep regular breathing, Katherine knew he was out of the woods.

"You're gonna make it, little fella," she said as she clutched him tightly to her chest.

After just a little while, Katherine realized she wasn't getting her arm back anytime soon. Whenever she attempted to put him down, so she could use it for another purpose, Odin would start crying and those cries would get louder and louder until she picked him up again.

As long as she held onto him, he was absolutely silent.

In fact, he was so silent that she would peek inside the blanket every couple of minutes, just to make sure he was doing alright, and of course… he was.

Realizing she was absolutely overwhelmed when it came to any kind of animals, she decided to play it safe and find help for Odin right away. Flipping through the internet results on her smartphone, Katherine found the address and telephone number of a local veterinary clinic. It was directly along her route to the office where she worked. In fact, she'd been driving past it for years without even realizing it was there.

Although there was a 24-hour emergency care number, the normal clinic hours were 7:00 a.m. to 7:00 p.m., so she decided to take a personal day from work to make sure the clinic where she was taking him would actually provide the care he needed. Considering all he'd been through, the last thing she wanted was for him to be abandoned or tossed off another bridge a few days from now.

After notifying her secretary she wouldn't be coming in, she made a pot of coffee and a toasted bagel, then checked her email accounts for any urgent matters. The entire time, Odin rested in the crook of her arm without a care in the world, his little ears and nose twitching imperceptibly as he absorbed his surroundings, subconsciously committing everything to memory.

Odin was home.

Chapter Two

Later that afternoon, with Odin securely wrapped in his blanket on her lap, and the shoebox on the passenger's seat beside her, Katherine drove to the Wilcox County Animal Shelter & Clinic just a few miles from her home. Being a no-kill facility, she was shocked and amazed at the callousness of someone who preferred to drown helpless pups rather than make the additional five-minute drive to a facility that would have taken them in and cared for them until they could be adopted.

In the parking lot outside the center, she was hopeful Odin could be adopted quickly, and become part of a family who would care for him and give him a great home. As a financial consultant for an investment brokerage, she told herself it would be impossible to give him the care he deserved.

She'd never been a pet owner before and hadn't the faintest idea as to how she should care for a dog. Her bags were still packed from her last trip, and the next one was only a few days away.

The cute little ball of black fluff was oblivious to her musings, as he slept soundly on her lap.

The walk across the parking lot toward the front door of the clinic seemed to go on forever. With the box under one arm and Odin under the other, she walked through the doorway with a heavy heart and placed the box on the countertop in front of her.

The young woman at the reception desk looked over the box into the distressed eyes of the woman behind it, and immediately knew the contents within. Although she'd seen that box in many different forms, shapes, and sizes over the years, the pain in the eyes behind it was always unmistakably similar.

Without a word, she carefully removed the box from the counter, carrying it into one of the examination rooms behind her. When she re-emerged, she approached Katherine, taking her hand. "I'm very sorry for your loss," she said. "We'll take care of them for you."

"Thank you," replied Katherine. "I really didn't know where else to bring them," she added.

Looking down, the receptionist, her eyes widening, asked "And who is this little guy?"

Katherine explained her morning ordeal, and how this was the sole survivor, asking, "Do you think you can find a good home for him? He's already been through so much."

"Well, that will depend a lot on him. Let's take him back to an exam room and check him out."

"Thank you…?"

"Doctor Forrester," she replied. "I'm the Veterinarian here."

The examination showed that despite his low bodyweight, he was in relatively good condition overall.

She estimated the pup to be only two or three weeks old, mentioning, "It's astonishing he survived at all."

Dr. Forrester handed the yelping puppy back to Katherine, where he quickly settled down again as she left the room. When she returned, Dr. Forrester told Katherine the shelter supervisor was on the way up to get him and would be there in a couple of minutes.

A short time later, a woman, wearing green scrubs and a nametag bearing the name LINDA, entered the exam room. "I'm sorry it took me so long to get here." She explained, "We just found a home for an elderly German Shepherd who'd been here for almost two months. It's a little harder to find homes for larger breeds, but eventually we find a family for all of our fur babies."

Katherine chuckled, "Well, this little guy will be easy to find a family for."

"Not necessarily," Linda explained. "There's a difference between a small dog, and a small breed dog. This little guy looks like a mix between a black Labrador and another large breed… most likely a Pit Bull judging by the shape of its head. He may be small now, but odds are, he'll be a big friendly giant by the time he's two years old."

"Wow!" Katherine exclaimed. "I had no idea."

When she reluctantly handed the swaddled little bundle over to Linda, Odin awakened, protesting vehemently.

"You'd better go now," Linda said. "He's already fixed onto your scent, and as long as you're here, he'll continue to protest."

As the pup's cries became more and more intense, the tug on Katherine's heartstrings was unbearable. She ran out the door to her car with Odin's agonized voice still ringing in her ears. She sat there for nearly ten minutes, her head resting on her arms folded over the steering wheel, weeping.

"What's happening to me?" she said out loud, banging her hand against the steering wheel. "You're just a dog! I don't even know the first thing about taking care of you," she sobbed.

Katherine realized she was talking to a dog who wasn't even in the car with her. Still, it felt to her as if he was listening to every word.

"I wanted to be a good mother. I really did," she said, before realizing that she was no longer talking about Odin.

When she was younger, she'd wanted it all. The exciting career, the successful husband, and the child with the silver spoon. In her mind, she had it all worked out, and nature had nothing to do with it... until it did.

How many times had her doctor counseled her to take it easy, and to avoid stress which could complicate her pregnancy? "How hard can it be?" she'd say. "I'm the one doing all the work. All the baby has to do is sleep," she'd always say to her colleagues jokingly.

One night after finally reeling in an account she'd been courting for months, she wrapped up her video conference call, and headed home shortly before midnight. Her mind was already sipping that cup of spiced tea in front of her fireplace, and planning what to do with that big fat commission check.

She didn't see the sheet of black ice covering the road as she turned right, onto the old Gatwick Bridge.

Suddenly, the cement abutment was rapidly closing in on the door of her new Carrera, and there was nothing she could do to stop it. The impact left her unconscious inside a car dangling precariously over the side of the bridge, and although the emergency responders were able to save her with the jaws of life, they couldn't save her baby.

Katherine was crushed at the loss of her child. For months, she was inconsolable, blaming herself for pushing too hard and putting her career ahead of her family. Ironically, it was her career that she defaulted to in order to bury the pain she felt, even at the expense of her marriage.

Now, here she sat, heartbroken, after handing over a gift given to her from the very same bridge which had taken her unborn child.

"No!" she said. "Never again!"

After gathering herself and regaining her composure, Katherine resolutely strode back into the clinic. This time, when she returned to the car... so did Odin.

Chapter Three

As Odin grew, so did his appetite… not only for food, but for knowledge, exercise, and experience as well. Within a few weeks, he had graduated from bitch milk to puppy chow, and his eyes began to mature, revealing a deep amber hue. At seven months, while technically still a puppy, he was already enormous!

Katherine's morning jogs pushing him ahead of her in a doggy stroller were short-lived. Having long since abandoned the quest to beat her record time from a year ago, she was content spending the start of her days with her best friend and four-legged running mate.

Even after stopping to sniff and mark every tree, bush, large rock, and clump of grass, and chasing every rabbit and squirrel appearing along the wooded path into the underbrush with no real intention of catching them, and absolutely no sense of what he would do with one if he ever did… he was always waiting for her at the boat dock when she topped the final rise leading down to the house, and he would not budge until she'd safely reached the yard.

It became a challenge to Odin to see just how much of those woods he could explore, and still make it back to the dock before Katherine appeared at the top of the hill. As he got bigger, so did the swath of forest he could cover, until he knew every inch of ground, every tree, and every indigenous animal between the old Gatwick Bridge and Katherine's back yard.

Sometimes, Katherine would watch Odin dart into the woods ahead of her, then really kick it into high gear, increasing her speed and running as fast as she could, trying to reach the top of the hill before Odin could reach the boat dock. The closest she ever got was to catch him as he was sitting down and turning to face the hilltop just as she crested it. It happened once, then never again. Not because he felt she'd beaten him, but because he felt he'd not sufficiently protected her. In Odin's mind, his entire existence was dedicated to protecting her from dangers both seen and unseen.

For that, he needed to be faster, and stronger, and always ready to defend her at a moment's notice... regardless of the circumstances.

After Odin entered her life, Katherine decided she'd rather come home to her dog every day than spend her life flying around the globe chasing more money... something she already had plenty of.

Odin gave without even the expectation of a return, and his loyalty came not from a bag of savory treats but from actually wanting her approval and praise for things he'd done well. His emotional sincerity was something she was initially unprepared for, because no one had ever been as openly affectionate to her as Odin was.

During her occasional dates, while her suitors droned on and on about themselves, puffing their chests out and strutting around like audacious peacocks, Katherine would find herself comparing them to the quiet confidence and loyalty of her little puppy… who was neither a puppy, nor little anymore.

Odin had a keen sense of intuition, and at times, Katherine truly believed he could read her mind. The bond they shared was unbreakable, and it was amazing to watch the dynamics of their relationship and the energy shared between them.

With Odin, everything was either black or white. Either he liked you, or he didn't. Kids, tennis balls, waterlogged sticks, frisbees, other dogs, bacon (lots of bacon), and wallowing in foul-smelling puddles—he liked. Suspicious strangers, snakes, spiders, baths, and Dr. Forrester—he didn't, although Dr. Forrester was slightly less intolerable than a spider.

At the age of two, due to his size, Dr. Forrester recommended obedience training for Odin. It was something at which he absolutely excelled. Odin learned not only from watching what handlers were teaching him, but also from watching them while they trained other dogs in more advanced specialty areas. Often, by the time they got around to showing him something, he'd already learned it merely from watching other dogs do it.

When it came to performing training tasks, Odin always wanted to go first. That way, he could watch the advanced specialty training of the dogs in the Police K-9 field on the other side of the fence separating the two facilities, while the remaining dogs in his group worked to catch up.

On one occasion, having grown bored with sit, stay, roll over, and beg, Odin defiantly jumped the fence, after watching several of the police dogs fail to successfully negotiate the obstacle course, and discover the hidden reward… a doggie treat. He could smell the treats inside the officer's pocket, as well as the hidden one tucked inside the thermal blanket in the bottom of the shallow leaf-covered foxhole at the far end of the obstacle course. Running the entire course flawlessly without ever having actually been on that field before, Odin left the training officers dumbfounded.

It would have been one thing to simply run directly to the hidden prize at the end of the course, but Odin actually reveled in overcoming the obstacles along the way. It was as if he wanted to show everyone present, both human and canine, that for him, it was ridiculously simple, requiring only minimal effort on his part, to show up everyone else watching from the sidelines.

At the end of the course, he dragged the blanket out of the foxhole and unfolded it, revealing the treat, but made no attempt to eat it. Sitting proudly in front of his discovery, Odin waited patiently as the training officer approached from one side, and Katherine ran towards him from across the field on the other. She reached him first, taking a knee beside him in the grass.

"Odin, you can't just run off like that without letting me know," said Katherine, taking his huge head in her hands, pinching his cheeks like a doting grandmother.

"Bark, howl, or do something to give me a heads-up next time," she said seriously, looking him directly in his amber eyes.

Odin blinked as if to acknowledge her words, then she hugged him before they turned to face the approaching officer.

"That's some dog you've got there, ma'am!" said the training officer. "How long have you been training him?" he asked.

"This is our second time here," said Katherine. "Dr. Forrester recommended some basic obedience training for him, so we signed him up last week. He gets a little over-enthusiastic at times, but he doesn't mean any harm."

"He's obviously a quick study," noted the officer.

"He certainly loves a challenge," added Katherine.

"Do you think he'd be up for some more advanced courses? We teach things like personalized hand signals, near-silent whistle commands, aggressor takedown techniques, and stuff like that… if you're interested," stated the trainer. "It'll definitely be more challenging for him than training with Poodles and Pomeranians."

Katherine nodded in agreement, saying, "Yeah, I think you're right about that. When can we get started?" she asked.

"A new course starts next week," said the trainer. "Just sign up at the admin desk up front, and we'll get you both in on Monday," he added, walking back towards his training group. After a few steps, he stopped, turning to look back at Katherine and Odin, shouting…

"Hey!"

"Yes?" said Katherine, also looking back.

"Why didn't he eat the treat inside the blanket?" asked the trainer.

"It's called 'Search and Rescue,' not 'Search and Eat the Victim.' Right?" replied Katherine. "Besides… Odin hates salmon," she said smiling as she turned to continue on her way to the admin office. Odin was quite pleased with himself, darting back and forth, and bounding about like a deer, escorting Katherine as they crossed the grassy field back to the front of the canine training facility.

For him, there was no difference between "search and rescue," and "playing a game of fetch," and he quickly mastered everything because he was keenly aware of everything around him at all times. At the top of that list was Katherine, and Katherine... Odin loved.

Chapter Four

ODIN remembered everyone, whether he'd actually met them or not. His sense of smell was so keen, he could distinguish between the scents of a dozen different people in a confined space. He knew who was in a room, just as he knew who was not in that room. He knew who was nervous, who was menstruating, and who'd been smoking, even if their last cigarette had been days ago. He also knew who should be there… and who shouldn't.

In Odin's view, people very often changed their fur, sometimes several times each day. For him, it was pointless trying to recognize them based on their appearance. However, their smell was an altogether different matter. It was a mixture of chemistry and environment, diet and personal hygiene, and for Odin, it was as unique as a human fingerprint.

Katherine and Roger had divorced a full year before she adopted Odin. It had been even longer since they'd actually lived together. Still, Odin knew him. There were boxes in the basement with things inside them which still carried Roger's scent, however faint it may have been.

Roger and Katherine had married straight out of college, immediately diving into their careers without giving their budding marriage a real chance at survival. Their jobs kept them separated for long stretches of time, often on opposite sides of the Atlantic. Try as they might, they were unable to overcome the constant separation, which made them feel more married to their cell phones than to each other.

Their bank accounts grew, but their relationship slowly withered, and died... a casualty of their mutual success.

Roger was different than the other men who tried dating Katherine. There was no awkwardness between them, and Odin didn't feel the urge to kill him the second his foot hit the porch steps. He'd watch them hug and could recognize the genuine affection they had for one another. Odin decided he liked Roger... not as much as he loved Katherine, but enough to be happy when he'd come to visit.

Similarly, Roger was very comfortable around Odin. He was thankful for Odin's protective nature regarding Katherine. Since she lived alone on her private peninsula, Odin was the perfect deterrent for anyone seeking to approach uninvited.

Seven years after rescuing Odin, their morning jogs had become afternoon walks down to the old bridge. Katherine would toss his tennis ball upstream into the river where he'd leap in after it, intercepting it in time to drift downstream and exit the water a few feet from where she stood.

The old bridge had long since been condemned due to increased concerns over its structural integrity, and traffic was rerouted to a new bridge a mile further upstream. Still, the old bridge was an excellent spot to escape the summer sun and enjoy the shade it provided.

Most of the time, it was only the two of them... Katherine and Odin, but sometimes Roger would join them for their evening walks. Odin loved how Roger could throw the ball further upstream, making retrieval more challenging for him. Being part Lab, he loved the water in spite of it having nearly claimed his life as a pup.

There was no jealousy between Roger and Odin. They shared a mutual respect for one another, each of them accepting the roles they played in Katherine's life.

They became fast friends.

One afternoon, Katherine stayed behind, watching through the kitchen window as her two boys headed down the lane on their daily trek. She smiled as Roger threw the tennis ball to Odin's unending delight, and they both disappeared over the rise heading toward the old bridge.

There, in the shade of the bridge, Roger sat at the river's edge, patting the ground beside him. Odin came and sat next to him, ears perked and eyes sparkling.

"I know you understand me," Roger said. "I want to marry Katherine again, but she told me I'd need your blessing."

Silence followed as their gazes locked.

"Honestly, I don't blame her," he added. "You've been loyal to her for nearly eight years... much longer than I have, and you've never left her side."

They both sat there looking out at the sunlight dancing across the rippling surface of Willis Creek.

"We were too competitive," said Roger. "We were always trying to 'one-up' each other, seeing who could get the better deal, or the biggest client, or the most impressive bonus check. Even when we were expecting a child, we couldn't let go of our insane fixation with winning, even though we already had everything," he said.

Odin sat patiently, listening as Roger explained, perhaps not understanding every word, but feeling the burden Roger was trying to lift from his shoulders. A burden he'd been carrying for far too long.

"I thought a baby would bring us closer, and it probably would have, had I not been such a moron."

Roger continued. "I was only joking when I told her she couldn't keep up with me anymore when it came to landing those big fish." Looking at Odin, he said, "I actually danced around the bedroom in my boxers, singing 'We Are the Champions' like an idiot." Shaking his head as if realizing the magnitude of his own stupidity for the first time, he said... "What the hell was I thinking?"

"After that, the gloves were off again," he said. "She was obsessed with winning, and no matter what I said or did, she wouldn't let up. Even though I'd promised her I'd work for all of us, so she could concentrate on taking care of the baby, and making the perfect home for our fairytale life, she wasn't having any of it. To her, it was all just a ruse, designed to make her let up so I could win."

"Are you getting all of this, buddy?" asked Roger, looking at Odin, who was still listening attentively.

"I wish I'd paid as much attention to her as you do," he said.

"After we lost the baby, she was so sad. I'd never seen anyone that utterly broken before, and I knew it was all my fault," Roger continued. "She said she didn't blame me, but I always felt she did. Eventually, it was my guilt, and her silence, that caused our relationship to wither on the vine and die, even though my love for her never did."

Stroking the pitch-black fur of Odin's powerful neck, Roger said, "I'm still in love with her, Odin, and I would really like to spend the rest of my life with you guys. Do you think we can manage that?"

The two of them sat there quietly beneath the bridge.

Odin could feel the enormous weight that had been lifted from Roger's shoulders by his confession, and laid his massive head on Roger's thigh, as if to reassure him everything would be alright.

Closing his amber eyes, Odin enjoyed the sound of the water rushing past, the earthy smell of the muddy shores along the creek bed, and the strong hand rubbing his head and neck.

It had been hours since they'd set out for their afternoon walk, and by the time they topped the rise leading down to the house, Odin could see Katherine sitting beneath the light of the front porch, with the smell of fried chicken and cornbread rushing out to meet them as they made their way down the lane.

Upon reaching the house, Odin sat at the foot of the steps while Roger continued onto the porch, taking Katherine in his arms and kissing her. After a long moment, the kiss ended, and Roger said, "I believe he said yes."

Looking over Roger's shoulder at Odin sitting calmly in the front yard, Katherine asked, "Any missing limbs or digits?" Backing away, she unceremoniously patted him down, as if to make sure.

"Nope. Still all in one piece," said Roger, smiling.

"Then I guess that piece is all mine," said Katherine, putting her arms around his neck and kissing him again.

The bond between the three of them was now complete, and Odin was happy as he rushed up the steps past them into the house… where the fried chicken and cornbread had been waiting for far too long.

Chapter Five

In the days and weeks that followed, a lot of things began to change. Roger was with them nearly every day, and Katherine was happy in a way she hadn't been in a very long time… since as far back as Odin could remember anyway.

Odin was also excited, as boxes arrived with more things inside them that smelled like Roger. In one of them was an amazing stick, the likes of which Odin had never seen. It was long and smooth, and thicker on one end than it was at the other. Roger kept it in the corner behind the front door. Looking at Odin, he said, "This is for just in case." Odin was anxious to see just how far Roger could throw that stick, certain he could fetch it with no problem.

There were boxes with clothes and shoes and papers and pots and pans and pictures of Katherine and Roger together. A few of the grey streaks were missing from Katherine's hair, and Roger had put on a few extra pounds, but they were smiling the same way they did every day since Odin's walk with Roger down to the bridge.

One of the most amazing things for Odin was Roger's pickup truck. A car where Odin could ride outside while Roger and Katherine rode inside. How amazing was that?!

And then there was the big party! Everyone Odin knew was there, including the little girl from the park who called him Pony Dog. They played music, and Katherine came out of the house with her dad and joined him and Roger and everyone else near the dock at the river's edge. There were sights and sounds and food and smells galore, and Odin's nose captured and categorized each and every one of them.

After the party, things slowly got back to normal again, and life with Katherine and Roger was peaceful and wonderful. They went everywhere and did everything together, but the highlight of Odin's day was still his evening walk with Katherine and Roger.

Odin would always run ahead, clearing the path of all rabbits and squirrels, and searching for waterlogged sticks along the muddy banks, that Roger could throw into the water for him to fetch. They had to be just the right size. Big enough to get a good grip on, but not too heavy for Roger to toss far out into the water.

They were nearly at the new bridge when Odin found just the perfect stick! He was proudly trotting back toward Katherine and Roger with it when he suddenly froze in his tracks. There was something unusual in the air which caught Odin's attention. Lifting his huge head into the air, nostrils flaring wildly, and ears perked, Odin went on full alert!

It only took a moment for him to isolate the scent in the air, then he turned his head toward Katherine and Roger, and did something he rarely ever did. He barked.

Odin's bark came from a deep place. It resonated within his massive chest and erupted from him like a muted explosion. Carrying along the banks of Willis Creek, it could easily be heard for miles.

Katherine had only rarely heard Odin's bark. Roger had never heard it, and it was terrifying!

"What is it, boy?" Roger replied.

Once again, Odin's bark resonated throughout the hallow as he bolted into the woods. He knew exactly where he was headed, and his legs couldn't carry him fast enough. The smells guiding him were all well known. The decaying trunk of the fallen oak, the mosquito-infested sinkhole filled with stagnant, foul smelling water, the thorny clustered hedge of wild roses... and Pony Dog Girl!

Odin ran faster.

Crashing through the ever-darkening woods, his bark illuminating the way for Katherine and Roger who were lagging far, far behind, he finally reached the fallen oak. Running along the top of the decaying trunk, Odin leapt the rose hedge, landing mere inches from the edge of the dank sinkhole.

His bark became more and more desperate, as Roger and Katherine called after him. They were still so far behind, and Pony Dog Girl was down there in that God-awful hole!

Seconds later... Odin was too!

There was literally no room for Odin to stand in the bottom of the death pit. By sheer luck, Pony Dog Girl's left arm and wrist had been wedged between two large stone outcroppings in the steep muddy walls of the sinkhole, about two feet above the rancid water. It was badly broken, but it was also the only thing keeping her from being swallowed completely by the dark, murky water.

Odin had been swimming in circles through debris and rotting animal carcasses in near total darkness, looking for a place to climb out of the water. There was none. However, directly beneath the little girl, he discovered a small shelf about four feet below the surface.

Diving under the thick oily water, he came up beneath her... her legs straddling his neck. Standing on the shelf using his hind legs, he placed his front paws against the slick wall of the sinkhole and was able to lift most of her little body out of the water by wedging himself upward between her and the wall.

As he extended his hind legs, she slid slowly down his neck, and came to rest straddling his broad back. He felt her right arm grabbing onto his neck, and her little hand gripping his fur. She held onto him tightly... like a pony.

Odin began to bay upward, toward the mouth of the sinkhole. He knew Katherine was out there, and that she would come for him... She would always come for him.

Odin's eerie howls resonated throughout the dark woods.

But for his baying, everything in the forest was dead silent.

Using her cell phone, Katherine was on hold with the sheriff's office for what seemed like an eternity! When the deputy finally answered, he explained all of the phones had been rerouted to their amber alert tip lines, which had been ringing off the hook since Isabel Mason was abducted from the park earlier that afternoon.

Suddenly, she understood. "Odin found her!" Katherine exclaimed.

"What?" replied the deputy.

"Odin has found her!" Katherine repeated.

"Your dog, Odin?" he responded.

"Yes!" Katherine screamed. "He is with her now!"

"Where are they?" asked the deputy.

"They're a mile or so into the woods west of the New Gatwick Bridge," Katherine flatly stated.

"And how exactly do you know this, Mrs. O'Connor?" asked the deputy, warily.

"Stick your head out a goddamned window!" she screamed. "He's telling me... He's telling everyone where they are!"

Odin was tired. He had run nearly two miles into the woods at full gallop to reach the sinkhole. Once there, he'd plunged into the pit and swam for several minutes looking for a ledge upon which he could pull himself and the little girl out of the filthy water. The submerged ledge he stood on was very narrow, and very slick, and it took everything within him to hold his position against the slippery wall.

His bellowing howl continued ceaselessly, reverberating from the walls of the pottery-jar-shaped crater where it was amplified as if from a megaphone.

Katherine stayed on the phone with the deputy, transmitting her GPS coordinates to his cellphone as she and Roger made their way through the dark woods.

Using the flashlight app on his smartphone, they fought their way through the thicket of wild roses.

Pushing through the hedge, Roger nearly stumbled into the sinkhole himself. Luckily, Katherine grabbed hold of his jacket, pulling him back from the crumbling rim at the very last instant.

As they cautiously peered over the edge with Roger's flashlight, they were at once relieved and horrified at what they saw. Isabel was clinging to Odin's neck... his forepaws

33

pressed firmly against the muddy wall, and claws dug in deeply. From his ribcage down, he was submerged in the wretched black water, and his entire body was trembling.

"Hang on, Odin! Mama's here!" Katherine shouted into the sinkhole. "We're gonna get you two out of there, big boy!"

Suddenly, there were lights, and voices, and sirens and ropes and ladders, and people everywhere. Rescuers carefully freed the little girl's broken arm from between the rocks, and gently lifted her from Odin's back and into the sky above.

Odin was already displaying signs of hypothermia from being submerged for so long. He couldn't even feel his legs anymore when they attached the harness around his torso and lifted him from that deadly black hole.

Katherine and Roger were waiting for him as he cleared the top of the crater. Behind them were dozens and dozens of people, cheering and clapping as they carefully lowered Odin onto a gurney and guided him into an ambulance from the Wilcox County Animal Shelter & Clinic.

While Dr. Forrester personally strapped Odin in, Katherine and Roger joined them in the back of the ambulance. Roger's arm was around Katherine's shoulder as she stroked Odin's giant muddy head. On the other side of him, Dr. Forrester started an I.V. drip, then covered Odin with a warm heavy blanket.

Animal clinic ambulances are neither equipped with, nor authorized to use sirens when transporting injured pets. That small detail didn't matter much to the sheriff's motorcade escorting Odin. Their sirens blared on defiantly, clearing a path worthy of a hero, all the way to the front door of the clinic, and the eager staff anxiously awaiting Odin's arrival.

Katherine leaned in close to Odin, taking his dirty, lovable face in both of her hands. As he started to drift off, he heard her whispering to him. "Good boy, Odin… Good, good boy."

Odin slept.

Chapter Six

The next morning, Odin awakened in the recovery room of the clinic. Katherine was asleep in a makeshift bed on the floor beside him, and Roger was just walking in with bagels and hot coffee.

Odin attempted to sit up, but he was still heavily sedated, and his hind feet were thickly bandaged.

Whatever he'd been standing on in that sinkhole had been cutting into his paws the entire time. He'd lost a lot of blood, which had substantially weakened him, causing the dangerous drop in his body temperature and uncontrollable shaking.

With the help of her medical staff, Dr. Forrester had bathed him and attended to his wounds. Through the night, he'd been on a saline and antibiotic I.V. to help rehydrate his body and fight off any infection he may have contracted from exposure to, and ingestion of, the contaminated water in the sinkhole.

Keeping him wrapped in an electric thermal blanket, Dr. Forrester was able to gradually raise his body temperature, preventing him from slipping into shock.

Katherine remained with Odin the entire time, not resting until Odin's condition had been stabilized and he was resting peacefully. Roused by the smell of the fresh coffee and bagels, she was surprised but delighted to see Odin was awake. His eyes were a bit glazed, but his big pink tongue bathed her face in wet kisses as she leaned over and nuzzled against him.

A few minutes later, Dr. Forrester entered the room wearing the white lab coat Odin had always perceived as a warning he was about to be poked and prodded again.

This time, he seemed un-bothered by it. He even licked her hand as she reached out to him, closing his eyes while she scratched him behind his ears.

Most of the events of the previous day faded quickly for Odin. Once the anesthesia had worn off, his appetite returned with a vengeance... much quicker than his memory did. Although the thick layers of gauze and padded dog boots on his hind feet felt awkward to him, before long he seemed to get the hang of it.

After a few hours of close observation, and a strong course of antibiotics, Dr. Forrester released him to go home.

Upon exiting the clinic, Odin was met by the cheers and applause of dozens of well-wishers, along with the flashing lights and cameras of the local news crew. A reporter thrust a microphone in Katherine's face, asking "How does it feel to know your dog is a local hero now?"

"Odin has been a fighter and a special part of our family since the day we met," Katherine said. "For him, it was just the right thing to do, and he reacted instinctively. It's something any compassionate person would have done, had they been in the same situation."

"Well, there you have it folks. Straight from the hero's mom," said the reporter, turning and looking into the camera as Katherine and Roger loaded Odin into the back seat of the car to head home.

As usual, Odin stuck his head out the lowered window, taking in the sights and smells of the town as they drove through. When they topped the rise leading down to their house, there were dozens of small white paper bags illuminated from within by glowing tea light candles, lining both sides of the long narrow lane.

Once they'd parked, Katherine and Roger helped Odin out of the car and into the living room, where he curled up happily in his favorite spot—the warm hearth of the fireplace.

Still, there was something he needed to remember.

Something important. It would surely come back to him if he could only block out the effects of the pain medication and fatigue of the past 24 hours.

The familiar sounds and smells of home, Katherine pouring hot water over little bags of jasmine and spice tea in the kitchen, the crackling embers of a fire slowly burning down, and the peaceful, never-ending flow of Willis Creek outside as it rushed to join the river beyond, all combined to relax and soothe him. By the time Katherine returned to the living room with hot tea for herself and Roger, Odin was sound asleep.

Katherine sat next to Roger on the couch, glad she could finally put her feet up, and breathe that sigh of relief she'd been holding in since the previous night.

Sinking into the couch with Roger's arm around her shoulder, the harrowing ordeal from the previous night seemed absolutely surreal to her.

"Did last night really happen?" she asked.

"It does seem like it was all a horrible dream," Roger said, leaning over and kissing her forehead.

"But, the reality is, there is still someone very dangerous out there, and until they catch him, we all need to be vigilant and cautious. It could be a total stranger, or someone we actually know."

"That's... that's just too disturbing to even think about," said Katherine. "The thought that someone we know could have possibly done this to a little girl... that's horrifying!"

Together, they sat there in comfortable silence, staring into the fireplace and digesting the events of the night before.

"He's amazing," said Roger, nodding toward Odin who was sleeping deeply. "Had he not found her..."

"Shhh..." interrupted Katherine. "I don't even want to think about it."

"How did he know?" asked Roger. "She was nearly two miles into the woods when he took off."

"These are Odin's woods," said Katherine. "He's been exploring this forest since he was old enough to lift his leg and pee on the trees."

Turning toward Roger, she asked, "Have you ever noticed that there are no snakes around the house, or anywhere on the entire property?"

"What do you mean?" asked Roger.

"Snakes..." repeated Katherine. "There used to be a ton of them around here. Cottonmouths, copperheads, rattlers, coral snakes... they were the reason I never left the jogging path on my morning runs. I'm terrified of them."

"Now that you mentioned it..." noted Roger.

"One morning, we were headed out for our run, and there was a rattler right there in the front yard at the bottom of the porch steps," Katherine continued.

"Normally, by the time I'd set the alarm code and stepped out on the porch, Odin was already halfway up the lane. That morning, he was still sitting at the top of the steps, and when I tried to walk around him, he wouldn't let me. That's when I heard the rattlesnake," she said.

"Odin was barely two years old, and it was the first time he'd ever seen me afraid of anything," Katherine recalled. "I literally screamed like a little girl and ran back into the house!"

"I don't think I've ever heard you scream," said Roger, as if trying to recall an instance when she may have.

"Well," said Katherine, "that morning I did. I ran all the way through the house and back into the kitchen. Then, I sat on a barstool, pulled my feet up to the seat, and wrapped my arms around my legs," she chuckled.

Smiling at Roger, she asked, "Did I mention that I'm terrified of snakes?"

"It may have come up once or twice," he replied with a grin.

"Anyway," she continued after sipping her tea and placing the cup on the end-table beside her, "I called animal control, and they said they'd send someone out right away. By the time I'd gathered myself enough to venture back out onto the porch, both Odin... and the snake... were gone!"

"What happened?" asked Roger.

"I called out for him and he came galloping around the corner from the back yard. His mouth and paws were still wet, presumably from drinking out of the creek. Just then, I looked up and saw animal control coming down the driveway. They saw me standing on the porch, and got out of their truck slowly… cautiously checking the ground with each step.

"They were wearing those Kevlar chaps and gloves, and when they finally made their way up to the porch, there was no sign of the snake," said Katherine.

"The whole time, Odin was watching them with that curious 'Odin' look on his face," she said.

"Oh, yes," replied Roger. "That look that says you're about to find out something he already knows."

"That's the one," replied Katherine.

"A few minutes later, one of the guys came back to the porch saying they'd found something, so I went with him to check it out."

"Laid out on the boat dock was this four-foot long timber rattler as thick as your forearm!" Katherine said. "It was in near perfect condition, and the only thing missing was its head. That's when I noticed… it wasn't water on Odin's face and paws. It was blood from that snake!"

"What!?" exclaimed Roger.

"Yes!" said Katherine. "He killed it! He bit the head off, then laid it out on the boat dock for me as a present, I guess."

"I offered to pay the guys from animal control for coming out, but they told me if I gave them the snake, we could call it even," Katherine explained.

"Apparently, there's a market for the skins of venomous snakes, but as far as I was concerned… I just wanted it gone.

"Anyway, that was the last time I ever saw a live snake on the entire property. Not just in the yard, ANYWHERE on the property… from the creek, all the way up into the woods," Katherine said.

"He'd lay them out on the dock, and I'd call the guys from animal control to come pick them up. For a while, it seemed like they were here every day," she recalled.

"Eventually, it tapered off, because there simply weren't any more snakes around here."

"Were you ever afraid he'd get bitten?" asked Roger.

"Every day!" replied Katherine. "His total lack of fear scares the crap out of me, but you know Odin. Once he gets something in his head, there's no shaking him off of it."

As Odin lay there by the warm hearth sleeping, his mind was working on a piece of the puzzle yet to be solved.

Like the lingering smell of this morning's coffee and bagels on Roger's sweater, there was a clue left behind by the man who'd taken Pony Dog Girl. An unmistakable remnant attributable only to him.

The man had touched the one part of her that wasn't contaminated by the filth of the toxic sinkhole water… The wrist he'd broken while dragging her through the woods. He'd held onto it tightly for quite a while… long enough to leave the scent of his fear-leaching sweat on her, and that was the only fingerprint Odin needed.

It was what he'd been struggling to recall, and now, having committed it to memory, his mind, like the rest of Odin's battered body… could rest.

Chapter Seven

The night of the rescue, Sheriff Ward designated the sinkhole and the surrounding area as an active crime scene. Bilge pumps were brought in to drain the toxic cesspool and search for any evidence or possible clues which might help them solve the child abduction case.

To the relief of everyone involved, no human remains were found in the pit.

That being said, there was plenty of evidence of a human presence. Rolls of copper wire and tubing, used power tools, sheets of 4-foot by 8-foot corrugated tin, sealed and partially sealed containers of paint and thinners, and a variety of smaller hand tools were discovered in the sludge blanketing the floor of the pit.

The list of items removed from the sinkhole seemed to match perfectly with one submitted in an insurance claim filed nearly two years earlier by a housing developer who'd been the victim of arson.

Long before the fire, investors had begun to grow weary of the project, announcing they'd pull out if faced with further delays. Shortly thereafter, tragedy struck.

Based on the evidence at the time, investigators thought it was a case of construction site theft by scavengers who'd taken high-value construction materials and easy-to-carry hand tools, before torching the rest of the project and using the fire to cover their tracks. Finding no evidence to the contrary, the case had grown cold, so the insurance company closed the investigation and paid the claim.

Sheriff Ward had always been skeptical of the theft/arson theory. Stolen copper wire and tubing, although lucrative for thieves on the black market, were never a reason to burn an entire construction site to the ground. In general, claims for construction theft are paid quickly to ensure the projects can be finished on schedule.

In his opinion, there was simply no reason to take this drastic a measure to cover up such a common crime. Nevertheless, without substance to support his theory, Sheriff Ward was left with only his opinion.

"And you know what they say about opinions…" he always said. "Every asshole's got one."

Now, here he stood, looking over the very evidence he'd been denied before, and adding two previously missing pieces to the puzzle. First… other than Odin, almost no one had known about this hiding place before yesterday. Secondly, whoever dumped Isabel here most likely knew about the stolen goods, and probably about the arson as well. The likelihood of this being coincidence in the Sheriff's mind wasn't even worthy of consideration, and Isabel seemed to be another victim in an ongoing cover up investigation.

Isabel was also a fighter. Although she hadn't yet regained consciousness, her vital signs were improving.

In addition to the compound fracture of her left arm, she'd also suffered severe head trauma before being tossed into the sinkhole. Had Odin not found her when he did, her chances of survival would have plunged to absolute zero.

To those involved in the investigation, none of it made much sense. She'd been abducted, but she was still fully clothed. There were no signs that she'd been sexually molested, and except for her head injury, there were no other signs of physical assault which couldn't be attributed to her plunge into the sinkhole.

The question remained… Who would do this to a six-year-old child, and for what reason?

No one had seen any strangers approach Isabel at the park. Everyone there was known, and most of them were neighbors and family members; however, witness descriptions of the pickup truck seen fleeing the scene were vague and often contradictory. Isabel knew not to talk to strangers and would certainly have run to her parents or a supervising adult had she felt threatened or uncomfortable.

There were potentially answers to all of these questions locked within the mind of that sleeping little girl as she silently fought for her life beneath the shroud of a coma.

Isabel's parents David and Barbara Mason were tireless soldiers in their little girl's fight for survival.

Most of their time was spent at her bedside, hoping and praying for their daughter to awaken from this horrible nightmare. Their initial joy at finding her, morphed into the pain of helplessly watching her suffer, while never giving up hope that she'd soon open her eyes to find both of them there for her.

The sense of guilt weighed upon them both like a wrecking ball. How could they have let this happen? It was a family outing… one of the last sunny autumn days warm enough to enjoy the great outdoors before the cold of winter descended upon their sleepy little town.

Nearly everyone in the park was part of their extended family.

They were just finishing up and packing everything into the car when they noticed she was missing. Thinking she might have just wandered into the wooded area adjacent to the park, David jogged over to the picnic area they'd just vacated, calling out to her.

"Isabel... Come on, sweetie. Time to go home. It'll be getting dark soon."

A moment later, Barbara came up from behind, calling out, "Isabel, honey, come on... It's time to go!"

Their calls into the forest went unanswered.

Soon, Barbara became frantic, shouting at the top of her lungs. "Isabel! Isabel!"

Within seconds, they'd drawn the attention of a few other stragglers who'd been wrapping up their day in the park.

David raced into the forest, scouring the wooded hillside joined by half a dozen others. Before they could reach the crest, they heard an engine roar to life, and caught only a brief glimpse of the pickup speeding down the fire break road behind the park, kicking dust and gravel into the air, obscuring the view of those attempting to follow. When the dust settled, the truck and Isabel... were gone.

Word spreads quickly in a small town, and within minutes the Sheriff's office was inundated with calls triggering the county and statewide Amber Alert systems.

The clock was ticking. Time and the weather were against the rapidly organized search party. Once the sun disappeared behind the mountains, the temperature would drop 30 degrees within minutes. Within an hour, it would literally be freezing cold.

As darkness descended into the valley, they heard it.

Odin's agonized baying filling the cold night air, echoing through even the deepest hollows of the river basin. Everyone stopped, and with the exception of Odin's blood curdling howl thundering through the star-lit night, the forest fell silent.

The search party began moving toward the sound, fearing what they might find when and if they were able to reach it, when suddenly the baying stopped.

Seconds later, Barbara's phone began vibrating in her hand.

Looking down at the screen, she realized it was her sister, Katherine, calling!

Frantically, she answered, "Katherine…?"

"Barbara… She's safe! Isabel is safe!" Katherine said. "Odin found her!"

"Oh my God, Katherine! Where is she?" asked Barbara.

"They're transporting her to Wilcox County Medical Center right now. Meet them there as soon as you can!" replied Katherine. "I've just got to make sure Odin's alright, then Roger and I will be there as soon as possible."

Katherine and Roger didn't make it to the Medical Center at all that night.

Chapter Eight

As winter descended on Wilcox County, the days became shorter, the nights became colder, and Sheriff Ward's child abduction case stalled completely. Although volunteers and deputies had spent days combing the woods searching for clues which could shed some light on and advance the investigation, they'd found nothing of any consequence.

After ten harrowing days of uncertainty, Isabel regained consciousness to the profound joy and relief of everyone across the county. Due to her head injury, she was unable to remember much of the ordeal, which doctors assured her parents, might well be a good thing.

She remembered the picnic and playing in the park with some of the other kids who'd been there. She remembered holding onto Odin's fur, and how he flew them out of the water and up into the sky towards all the bright lights. Other than those mental snapshots, she had absolutely no recollection of the events which had transpired.

After two weeks in the hospital, Isabel was finally cleared to go home. Her doctor strongly recommended she be evaluated by a child psychiatrist, stating in no uncertain terms that those memories would return, and her parents needed to be very clear as to just how traumatic an effect they could have on her, if they were unprepared to cope with them when they did.

For the moment, David and Barbara were just happy to have their daughter back, but they wisely accepted the doctor's recommendation.

Odin quickly grew accustomed to the boots on his bandaged feet. Within a few days, he was almost oblivious to them being there, and felt ready to resume his daily walks with Katherine and Roger.

Nothing doing!

Since the day she snatched him out of the water as a pup, Katherine vowed Odin would never have to face that kind of fear or uncertainty ever again. She'd never even seen him injured or in pain. To her, he'd always been this larger-than-life, indestructible bundle of joy, and watching him suffer there in silence was heartbreaking for her.

Odin felt trapped, and even though Katherine and Roger were doing everything possible to keep him comfortable during his recovery period, not being able to leave the front- or backyards felt more like punishment to him.

He'd sit on the front porch gazing out across the lawn, watching deer and wild turkeys wandering in and out of the tree line at the edge of the property, and longing to run up the lane again to the gate and beyond.

Like a helicopter mom, Katherine diligently watched over Odin until she was convinced he was ready to (gradually) get back to his walking regimen. Due to Dr. Forrester's excellent care and Katherine's iron resolve, within a few weeks, Odin was feeling as good as new.

After a final checkup with Dr. Forrester, where she finally removed his boots and bandages, Odin left the clinic with Katherine and Roger. When they reached the pickup, Roger lowered the tailgate. For the past weeks, he'd been required to sit up front with them, and could only hang his head out of the passenger window.

Realizing he was now being allowed to ride in back again, the look on his face was priceless!

He leapt right into the bed of Roger's truck, placing his paws atop the cab and facing forward into the wind.

He literally towered over the cab of the pickup, watching the journey back home from his favorite vantage point. As the pickup crossed over the New Gatwick Bridge, Odin could already see the lane leading down to the house off in the distance.

When they approached the gate, Odin leapt from the bed of the truck, shaking the whole vehicle as he landed in the tall grass at the edge of the fence line.

Katherine and Roger watched, smiling, as Odin shot across the field at full speed, finally able to stretch out and run like he'd been yearning to do for the past couple of weeks. He easily outpaced them, as they headed down the lane. Running past the front porch onto the boat dock at the back of the house, Odin leapt far out into the rushing water in an arc that would've made any athlete proud. Swimming to shore downstream, he ran back onto the dock, shaking vigorously, creating a beautiful 360-degree spray of water droplets which glistened like diamonds as they flew from his pitch-black fur, backlit by the morning sun.

By the time Katherine and Roger parked in the driveway, Odin was lying in the middle of the dock, soaking in the warm rays of sunlight, as he'd been yearning to do for weeks. Even the smell of the bacon and eggs cooking in the kitchen wasn't enough to lure him back inside the house, and while Odin napped in silence, his ears and wet black nose wiggled and adjusted to take in the sounds and smells of the peninsula still so familiar to him, even after his temporary lockdown.

"I think he's trying to make up for a month of missed outdoor time in a single day," said Roger, watching him through the back-screen door.

"Well, I'd argue that point with you, but with Odin, anything seems possible," replied Katherine. "I've learned never to underestimate him. If HE thinks it's possible, it probably is."

When Roger looked out the back door again, Odin was gone... already far up on the hill at the tree line, chasing the deer and wild turkeys which had been taunting him for weeks, back into the forest at the property's edge. After re-establishing his territorial boundaries, he zigzagged his way down the grassy field from edge to edge, at times, disappearing completely in the tall yellow grass, making sure everything was as he'd left it.

Later that afternoon as they were about to depart on a short walk, a car appeared at the crest of the hilltop, driving slowly down the lane and parking in the driveway. David and Barbara got out, smiling ear to ear as they opened the back doors of their car.

On the driver's side, Isabel exited, making a beeline straight to Odin who was trotting in place, struggling to contain the joy he felt at seeing her. She rushed up and wrapped both arms (including the one with the bright pink cast on her wrist) around Odin's neck, pressing her face against his thick black fur.

"I love you Pony Dog," Isabel whispered, "and I don't care what they say. I know you really can fly."

As Odin and Isabel stood there, Odin noticed another little surprise... a Rottweiler puppy clumsily bounding toward them from around the other side of the car, all ears and paws, and pink tongue flapping.

"This is Chloe!" Isabel proudly exclaimed, then whispered into Odin's ear... "Maybe you can teach her to fly too!"

Chapter Nine

Winter came and went in Wilcox County, and between the Sheriff's investigation and the almost smothering press coverage of the abduction, Barbara and David had grown weary of the constant buzz surrounding them and Isabel.

For the most part, they avoided watching the local evening news as suggested by Dr. Wagner, Isabel's child psychiatrist. She felt that constant exposure to the media flood could prove counterproductive to Isabel's ability to cope with what had happened.

Still, there were nights when Isabel would awaken... screaming and crying out for help. During those episodes, she would often wet the bed, triggered by her nightmares. Having Chloe by her side seemed to lessen the frequency of those nocturnal panic attacks, and as spring turned to summer, Isabel and Chloe became inseparable.

The most difficult moment for both of them came when Isabel started first grade! Barbara walked her to the end of the lane with Chloe following close behind, waiting for the Wilcox County Elementary School bus to arrive. Barbara was waging her own internal battle the first time Isabel boarded that bus, and it was all she could do to keep Chloe from climbing those steps right behind her! The fact that they'd talked about it and gone over it a dozen times, did very little to lessen the impact for either Barbara, Isabel, or Chloe.

That day, and every school day that followed, found Chloe lying on the front lawn in the shade of the old oak tree, waiting for that big yellow bus to appear atop the hill about a quarter mile from the house. By the time the doors opened at the end of the lane, Chloe was dutifully sitting there, waiting for Isabel to disembark.

Their weekend family outings to the park were even greater enriched by the ever-watchful Odin. He and Chloe were so entertaining to observe as they frolicked and chased one another through the park in pursuit of tennis balls, random sticks, and Frisbees, with neither of them ever losing sight of Isabel.

Katherine and Barbara had always been close, but the events of the previous fall seemed to bring them even closer together than ever before. When Barbara and David needed someone to watch Isabel, it was always Katherine and Roger, who treated her as if she were their very own child.

As Barbara and David would both be out of town on business over the weekend, Katherine volunteered to pick up Isabel that Friday after school. Chloe was always excited to see Katherine's car pull up in the driveway, because she knew Odin was always with her.

Once she heard the key in the door lock, Katherine couldn't open the door fast enough!

When she did, Chloe literally leapt off the porch into the lawn at a full run, with Odin right on her tracks, as they burnt a path down the lane, each taking turns chasing the other energetically, before returning to the shade of the big oak tree to wait for Isabel's bus.

It had not been a good day for Isabel. Somehow the word had gotten out, and rumors began to spread about her abduction nearly a year ago.

Children can be cruel in their ignorance at times, and often that ignorance is further fed and inflamed by their parents. A careless statement here, a false judgment there, and suddenly the victim becomes the brunt of insensitive jests and pranks, thereby being further victimized for their own misfortune.

In a place like Wilcox County, the rumors among children can be more infectious than chicken pox. It had only been a few weeks since school began, but bullies waste no time in finding targets upon which to vent their own insecurities and anger. Andrew and Colin were such bullies, and today they had it in for Isabel.

It started in the cafeteria, when Andrew pushed ahead of her in line.

"Hey," cried Isabel, "I was here first! That's not fair!"

Andrew turned and said, "I heard you drink from the toilet. I'm not going after you, swamp girl!"

His friend Colin pushed ahead next, shoving her to the floor and chanting "Swampy... Swampy... Swampy..."

Soon, several other kids joined in, echoing the chorus started by Colin. "Swampy... Swampy... Swampy..."

Isabel was mortified and remained kneeling on the floor in sheer panic until the lunchroom monitor finally intervened. After stopping the chant and helping Isabel to her feet, Isabel ran from the cafeteria, taking refuge in the girls' restroom.

Sitting atop the toilet seat, she began to cry. She hadn't felt this alone since she was discarded in that sinkhole a year ago. Somehow that place still managed to haunt her, even after all this time.

Suddenly, she heard a soft knock on the stall door. It was the school guidance counselor, Miss Nichols.

"Are you alright, sweetheart?"

"Go away!" cried Isabel through her tears. "Nobody likes me."

"That's not true," replied Miss Nichols. "Lots of people like you."

"No, they don't! They all called me Swampy, and they think I drink toilet water," replied Isabel.

"What Andrew and Colin did was wrong, and we've called their parents," said Miss Nichols. "They've been suspended, and won't be back for two weeks."

"Really?" said Isabel, slightly opening the stall door to take a peek.

"Really!" said Miss Nichols, taking Isabel's hand and kneeling in front of her. "We don't tolerate bullies here, and their parents will have a lot to answer for."

Isabel even managed a little smile as Miss Nichols wiped the tears from her face and hugged her.

"The way we stop bullies is by standing up to them. Can you do that with me?" asked Miss Nichols.

"I guess so," said Isabel.

Miss Nichols straightened Isabel's clothing and brushed the hair from her face. Together they walked out of the restroom right past all the glaring faces and shamefully averted eyes.

As they were leaving the lunchroom, a girl from Isabel's classroom handed her an apple and a carton of milk.

"Hi. My name's Emily," she said. "You missed lunch, so I saved you some of mine."

"Thank you, Emily," she said, smiling. "My name's Isabel."

As their teacher led them down the hallway, Miss Nichols heard Emily saying, "Hey, let's sit together at lunch next week!" as the two of them disappeared around the corner, giggling, on their way back to the classroom.

Andrew's and Colin's parents had grown accustomed to having their boys sent home early from school. They were both already the kind of kids that result from the lack of proper upbringing and parental intervention.

For their parents, calling the boys bullies only meant that they were able to fend for themselves better than the other kids. In fact, they treated it as a badge of honor... a badge they intended to put on full display after school, at Isabel's bus stop.

Andrew's mother came to the school earlier that day to pick up both boys after the lunchroom incident.

Following the intense shouting match with their principal, she left the office in a cloud of expletives with her son and Colin in tow.

The anger she vented on them had nothing to do with their unacceptable behavior in school. No... it was purely a rant about how they had interrupted her "Stories" on television that afternoon. The moment they arrived at the house, she went back to her soap operas, and Andrew grabbed a paintball gun from the shed before he and Colin bolted down the road on their bicycles, vowing to get even with a younger girl who had done nothing to them and was wholly innocent regarding the behavior which had gotten them suspended.

Chloe saw them first as they rode over the hilltop and down the narrow road toward the bus stop. They merited no more than a cursory glance from the two dogs who were waiting for one thing, and one thing only… Isabel.

When the bus finally appeared at the top of the hill, the race was on! Chloe was the first to bolt. She accelerated like a rocket, jumping to a quick lead ahead of Odin, who, with his longer gait, was just hitting his stride. In the 300 yards from the tree to the end of the lane, Odin ran his way to a photo-finish with Chloe as they arrived nearly simultaneously at the mailbox, just as the bus was slowing to stop.

Chloe sat patiently as she did every day, waiting for the door to swing open, and for Isabel to appear. Odin was on a different mission. He ducked into the wooded area adjacent to the road, wondering why those two boys, who came over the hill earlier, were still hiding in the tall grass there. He decided to wait and see.

As Isabel exited, the door closed behind her and the bus drove off. That's when the two boys popped out of the grass.

"Hey, Swampy!" Andrew called out.

"There's no teacher to stick up for you now," added Colin.

Chloe instinctively stepped in front of Isabel as she backed away from the boys.

"I ain't scared of your dog, Swampy," declared Andrew as he raised a paintball gun, aiming it at Chloe.

The deep rumbling sound behind the boys stopped them in their tracks. By the time they turned to look, Odin had silently crept to within inches of them... his eyes narrow amber slits, and the fur along his spine hackled and standing on end. His teeth were bared as he stood motionless... waiting.

While the boys were focused on Odin, Isabel and Chloe turned calmly to walk back up to the house. When Andrew attempted to raise the paintball gun, Odin's growl intensified. Saliva was dripping from his mouth, and he looked as if he was sizing them up for dinner.

Andrew lowered the paintball gun, placing it on the ground and backing away from it... slowly.

Suddenly, Odin's demeanor changed. His menacing growl stopped, and he lunged forward, causing both boys to fall to the ground, unable to get out of each other's way. Without touching either of them, Odin pounced on the paintball gun, grabbing and crushing it between his powerful jaws before bounding off with it towards Isabel and Chloe, who were already halfway up the lane.

When Isabel looked back again, both boys had hastily mounted their bicycles, and were peddling for their lives back over the hill from whence they came.

On the porch, Odin dropped the mangled paintball gun at Katherine's feet, before dashing off to join Isabel and Chloe in the backyard. Of all the things Odin had brought to the house over the years, this was certainly unique.

Katherine picked up the paintball gun and put it in the closet next to the front door. She'd been inside making soup and a sandwich for Isabel during the incident out near the mailbox, and hadn't witnessed what actually occurred. She went about watering the houseplants and packed some things for Isabel and Chloe's weekend at her house.

As they were leaving the house, they noticed a pickup turning into the lane out near the mailbox. They all waited on the porch as the vehicle approached, then stopped behind Katherine's car. When the doors opened, Andrew and his father got out and walked up to the porch.

"Hello, ma'am," said Andrew's father, addressing Katherine. "My name's Albert Cage, and this is my boy, Andrew."

"Katherine O'Connor," responded Katherine. "What brings you out this way today, Mr. Cage?"

"Andrew here says your dog attacked him, and took something that belongs to me," responded the man.

Katherine knew he was lying. Odin was never the aggressor and most certainly would not have attacked a child just to steal something from them. Still, she was curious.

"And just what did he take, may I ask?" said Katherine.

"One of my paintball guns," answered Mr. Cage.

"Hold on just a moment," said Katherine, reaching into the closet by the front door to retrieve the gun. Then, looking at Isabel, asked, "Do you know anything about this, Isabel?"

Andrew, who had been sheepishly silent up to this point, looked at Isabel with sheer panic in his eyes, afraid she was about to punch holes in the story he'd told his father.

"Andrew and Colin were teasing me, and calling me names at school today," said Isabel. "Colin pushed me and I fell down, and then they both started calling me Swampy."

"Really…" said Katherine, arms folded, turning toward Andrew and his father.

"Is that true boy?" asked Mr. Cage, stepping over to face Andrew. "Did you push her down?"

"It is true!" exclaimed Isabel. "You can ask Miss Nichols. She said they got suspenders and had to go home early."

"You mean suspended?" asked Katherine.

"Yes, suspended," answered Isabel. "And then Miss Nichols said they had to go home early and couldn't come back for two weeks!"

Mr. Cage stood there silently fuming, staring at the young boy. Andrew did not dare look his father in the eye, and Katherine could tell he was terrified.

Turning toward Isabel again, Katherine asked curiously, "Just how did Odin get a hold of the paintball gun?"

"Andrew and Colin were hiding in the bushes when I got off the school bus today. They were gonna try to shoot me with it, but Chloe wouldn't let them," said Isabel.

"Then they were gonna try to shoot Chloe with it too, and Odin wouldn't let them do that either, so they dropped it and ran away."

"Well, Mr. Cage, I guess that pretty much explains everything," said Katherine reaching out to hand him the mangled paintball gun. "If either Chloe or Odin had attacked your son, he'd look like this thing does."

Without warning, Mr. Cage forcefully backhanded Andrew across the face, knocking him hard into the side of Katherine's car, where he crumbled and fell to the ground. Reaching down and picking up Andrew by the collar of his shirt, he drew back with a clenched fist, ready to deliver another blow to the cowering little boy.

"Not only are you a lying little shit," shouted Mr. Cage. "You're a sniveling coward to boot!"

Before he could deliver the punch, Katherine stepped up, locking her arm in the crook of his elbow to prevent him from following through. Letting go of Andrew's shirt, he blindly jabbed behind him, striking Katherine in the cheek with his elbow.

When he turned to look back, Chloe was on the porch, standing in front of Isabel, growling. Katherine was on the ground covering her left eye with her hand, and Odin was in mid-air, two feet from Mr. Cage's chest.

The impact of a 140-pound dog crashing into his chest pounded Albert into the ground as if he were made of straw, knocking him out cold.

When he opened his eyes, Odin was standing over him, six inches from his face. His eyes were mere slits of amber behind a furrowed snout, baring teeth capable of ripping him to shreds. Beyond Odin, peering over his shoulder, was Katherine, looking down at the both of them.

"Now would be a great time for you to get the hell off of this property," stated Katherine flatly.

As Odin backed away from him, Mr. Cage scooted along the ground on his back to add some space between the two of them before scrambling to his feet. He hustled toward the still open door of his pickup, calling out to Andrew, "Come on, boy!"

"Andrew's going to be staying with us for a while," said Katherine adding. "At least until child protective services arrive."

"This ain't over!" sneered Mr. Cage.

"Oh, you're right about that," stated Katherine. "Tick-tock, Mr. Cage. You may even make it home before the Sheriff catches up with you."

With that, the angry man got into his truck and backed all the way out the driveway, kicking up dust and gravel like a petulant child who'd just lost all his marbles. Katherine took Isabel and Andrew back into the house, while Odin and Chloe remained on the front porch, guarding the door like the lions at the MGM Grand.

"I'm sorry about your dad," said Isabel, looking at Andrew.

"Step-Dad," said Andrew. "He's not my real dad."

"Are you hungry?" asked Isabel. "Auntie Katie made some soup and sandwiches. Would you like some?" Looking back and forth between Isabel and Katherine, Andrew didn't really know what to say.

"It's okay," said Katherine, pulling out a chair at the kitchen table for him.

Nodding timidly, Andrew took a seat across from Isabel. He looked around, taking in everything while Katherine re-heated the soup and took bread, cheese, and smoked ham from the refrigerator to make him a sandwich.

"I'm sorry, Isabel," said Andrew. "What I did to you wasn't nice, and I'm really, really sorry."

Looking down at the table, Andrew continued... "I always let Colin talk me into things, otherwise he beats me up. Then when I go home, my step-dad beats me up again and calls me a sissy."

When he looked up, there were tears in his eyes. "I just don't know what to do," he said, as his eyes pooled over, and tears ran down his face. "He beats me every day, no matter what I do."

It was as if a floodgate had been opened, and he completely broke down, weeping uncontrollably. Isabel stood up and walked around the table. Pushing a chair closer, she sat next to Andrew. "You can be my friend," said Isabel. "And you won't have to beat up anyone."

"Okay," said Andrew, smiling as he wiped the tears from his eyes.

Katherine, who'd been listening the entire time, had to wipe tears from her own eyes before placing the sandwich and bowl of soup on the table in front of Andrew. He dug in, wolfing everything down quickly, making Katherine wonder if the school lunch might be his only meal for the entire day.

"Cookies and milk for dessert anyone?" asked Katherine.

"Yes, please!" came the simultaneous reply from Isabel and Andrew.

While the kids ate dessert and played video games in the den, Katherine finally made the calls to Sheriff Ward, and Child Protective Services.

Chapter Ten

Autumn in Wilcox County was marked by the vibrant red and gold foliage in the crowns of the trees, spattered across the landscape and blanketing the forest floor.

The sun retires behind the mountains early, and the brisk chill in the air hints at the coming of winter.

Fireplaces are once again stoked to life, and the aroma of hearty meals being prepared in homes across the community is comforting and inviting.

Odin loved lying in those quickly fading sunny spots, soaking up the remaining rays of light as they broke through the colorful canopy of the trees overhead.

Without moving, his eyes would follow the wildlife inhabiting the forest. Rabbits and squirrels foraging for food on the leaf-covered ground would often come within mere feet of him as he lay there silently observing them.

There was so much to see from his vantage point, and all life in the forest paraded magically before him, as long as he remained perfectly still and silent. To all the creatures around him, he was just another random shadow on the ground; however, even when sunbathing, Odin was ever-alert… his ears perked, and his cold black nose filtering and analyzing every scent in the cool October air.

Katherine, although semi-retired, would still occasionally work from home. She maintained a small but active client base, which, at times, was too much for her taste. Having narrowly avoided a huge financial loss a few years back on a local real estate investment which ended in a months-long investigation over money laundering and suspicions of insurance fraud, she'd lost the taste for cultivating high-risk, high-yield investments, preferring a more moderate portfolio of mid-to-long-term options.

After being intensely audited for nearly two years by the United States Securities and Exchange Commission, she was exonerated on all counts, but the bad taste in the mouths of a few of her investment partners persisted even up to that day. They felt she should have done more in the way of developing other potential high-yield investment opportunities, which could possibly flip their losses from the previous project into large capital gains on a future one.

If Katherine had learned anything over the past 30 years, it was to stick to your exit plan on an investment. Get out of it once your profit or loss limits have been reached, and NEVER throw "good" money after "bad." In her experience, "Hail Mary" actions seldom produced favorable results, and more often than not, exposed investors to even greater losses.

Her instincts were proven correct, when she exited the project to cut her losses. Afterwards, the remaining partners mounted a futile attempt at a real estate venture which failed miserably, costing them millions of dollars, which could easily have been avoided had cooler heads prevailed.

That was truly Katherine's turning point. After that project, she scaled her career back dramatically, opting to avoid the strokes, heart attacks, nervous breakdowns, and suicide attempts which were all too commonplace in the world of finance and investments. It was a decision she'd never regretted.

Although Roger had also scaled back his workload, he'd still fly out on the occasional business trip as a consultant, or for paid speaking engagements around the country.

Such was the case this particular week. Roger was in sunny San Diego, while Katherine and Odin were bracing for the season's first snowfall. Earlier that morning, Katherine received a call from Maxwell, a former colleague, hoping to recover copies of some documents he required for an IRS audit. Although Katherine offered to email the documents to his office that afternoon, he explained he'd be in town anyway and would be happy to swing by and pick them up personally.

Besides, having last seen her and Roger at their wedding over a year ago, it would give them a chance to catch up.

Katherine agreed.

Maxwell was not the type of person who'd stand out in a crowd, either positively or negatively. He was always appropriately dressed, no matter what the occasion; however, when surrounded by men in $3000.00 custom tailored suits, his $1500.00 suit wouldn't betray the fact that he was actually trying incredibly hard to hang onto the very bottom rung of the social ladder he so desperately wanted to be a part of.

His pseudo-intelligence was more often a plagiarized regurgitation of facts he'd heard from someone else, often only moments after hearing them. He was a social chameleon, varying his pitch and presentation to favorably influence whoever was currently in front of him. During that first encounter with him, he would seem knowledgeable and attentive, but when you started to dig down, the shallowness of his persona became obvious to anyone with even a basic understanding of the facts being discussed.

It was easier for Maxwell to interact with others when he could blend into the crowd, waiting for the opportunity to recite his well-rehearsed lines for maximum impact. To the casual observer, he appeared to be a quiet, yet important element of a cohesive team.

In reality, he was more often the weasel waiting for the foxes to appear, so he could steal a chicken and blame them for it.

His drive was based on envy of, and hatred for, those who genuinely earned the respect of their colleagues by delivering on their promises. In fact, he spent more time trying to game the system than he did actually learning how to operate inside of it. Only by limiting his own exposure was he able to remain inside the circle he was so woefully unqualified to inhabit.

So many times, Maxwell had bet on the wrong horse when it came to investment opportunities, thinking he was ahead of the curve when actually he was far behind it. Always looking for an easy cash-out, he'd risked away a real fortune, by chasing imaginary ones.

A few times, when it looked like he'd finally get a deal across the finish line, it was his own lack of research, and inattention to detail, that were ultimately his undoing. Such was the case with the land investment deal he'd presented to Katherine five years ago.

Due to the county's push to encourage corporate development, they were offering huge incentives for investors in the tech sector, with the hope that the jobs created would be a boon to their local economy and put them on the national and international maps.

After pitching and selling the project, and having several big money investors pledge their support and financial backing, Maxwell was knocking on the door of the $3000.00 suit club. A club in which he did not want to be the smallest fish in the pond.

Luckily, there are always foreign investors hoping to sink their rabid teeth into purchasing property and influence in the United States. As a result, they were constantly looking to recruit partners who could give their dealings at least the appearance of legitimacy.

Unfortunately, these are not the kinds of people any reputable firm would want to have financially connected to them. Their dark, dirty money… while as abundant as sand on the beach, always came with conditions written in blood. Screw them over, and your life expectancy can often be measured in minutes.

For this project, Katherine's involvement was key, because her client list was generously populated with legitimately situated billionaires who could literally finance the entire enterprise with their petty cash accounts. They depended on Katherine to negotiate their deals and to make sure their investments would indeed generate serious returns.

After studying the proposal, verifying the county's tax breaks and subsidies in-depth, gaming out profit and loss projections, calculating how long it would take for those projections to go from red to black, and providing realistic returns on the investments of her clients, Katherine was actually impressed with the project to the point that she, herself, was willing to put up some of her own money, just to be a part of it.

The project would essentially be a technology campus, where some of the most pioneering individuals in the tech sector could be recruited to create a new Silicon Valley, right there in Wilcox County. Their contracts would include housing, which would allow them to live on-campus with their families, and a fleet of electric vehicles employees could use at their discretion for those occasions when they did need to venture beyond the grounds of the campus.

All of the on-campus facilities, including housing accommodations, would be securely interconnected through an independent autonomous network. There would be automated transportation throughout the campus via magnetic rail, eliminating the need for personal transportation, and 100% healthcare coverage for every employee and their family... regardless of whether they lived on campus with the employee or not.

Since the impact on their infrastructure would be significant, these healthcare benefits would be extended to every resident of Wilcox County, because in theory, all of them would be contributing to the support and success of the technology campus, and the jobs would pour in.

The company had already been registered as a C-Corporation, with the option of trading shares in stock markets around the globe under the name WILCO-TECH.

Based on the existing and pending patents already secured by the corporation in advance of the groundbreaking, the monetary potential was staggering.

Even the engineering and technology which would be applied in building the campus was already protected as the intellectual property of WILCO-TECH, and kept highly confidential.

Since Maxwell's investment group had already acquired the property and the access rights, Katherine was convinced this would be one of the most technologically advanced communities in the world within seven years, turning huge profits much, much sooner than that.

Having reviewed the 3-D architectural renderings, and conducted numerous flyovers to survey the campus location, Maxwell jumped at the opportunity to make the billion-dollar investment using the money he was confident would generate huge returns for his investors, and a life-changing influx of clean money for himself.

One would think every angle had been considered before Maxwell pulled the trigger on this massive land acquisition. As Katherine would soon discover, they had not. In her typical, methodical, boring, cover-all-the-bases evaluation, she discovered something aerial surveillance and 3-D architectural renderings had missed. Karst.

Looking deeper into the geologic maps and records provided by the county commissioner's office, Katherine came across the hand-written notes of a former forestry service surveyor, indicating the presence of karst subsidence, (a primary factor and contributor to the development of sinkholes), and the entire construction zone was riddled with it.

Karst is a type of soluble evaporative rock which, when exposed to the underground springs and cumulative rainfall of the mountainous regions in and around Wilcox County, could give way without notice or warning. The handwritten journal provided a detailed compilation of the areas affected, noting that sinkhole development was impossible to predict, and it was inevitable.

It was with a very heavy heart that Katherine laid out these findings for her investment group, admitting there was a chance that the appearance of these sinkholes could lie decades in the future. It could also be a week from now, or an hour from now. Even the experts were unsure, saying it was impossible to predict.

Her investors were so captivated by the idea of a technology campus, they were even willing to pay for seismic testing to see if there was a chance the journal had exaggerated the dangers it had outlined. Towing in the seismic thumper truck on a flatbed trailer and negotiating the narrow fire break roads up to the site, was an ordeal all its own. It was late evening when they finally arrived at the test location, and due to the fading daylight, the test was scheduled for the following day.

By the time the evaluation team returned to the test site the next morning, both the hauling rig and seismic thumper had been swallowed up and were lying on their sides in the bottom of a twenty-foot deep sinkhole. The driver of the rig was sitting on the passenger-side door, staring up at them, having climbed out through the window hours earlier.

Katherine, and the rest of her investment group, pulled their financial backing for the project immediately, effectively killing the project in its infancy. Adding insult to injury, the land value plummeted, leaving Maxwell horribly upside down on a piece of property with which he'd never be able to recoup his investment.

With the exception of the housing units which would serve as residences for the advance construction crew and property managers... which had also been funded by Maxwell's investment group... there was nothing to show for the financial exposure he'd allowed himself to be saddled with, and, due to the highly visible failure of the sinkhole test, there was no way to hide the fact that the land was essentially worthless.

On the other hand, Katherine's group was able to walk away, relatively unscathed, and aside from the seismic testing she'd ordered for them, their only financial commitments were to Katherine for her research and evaluation, which had undoubtedly saved them billions of investment dollars.

Based on the optimistic preliminary calculations provided by Katherine, Maxwell's tendency to jump the gun had landed him in a perilous position with a group of shadow investors who could make the remainder of his life short and miserable.

Within hours, the phone call he had been so looking forward to, became one he dreaded and feared. When it came, as he knew it would, the false optimism in his voice did little in the way of reassuring those whose money he'd so quickly and obviously squandered.

The discussion was short, ending with a single ultimatum. He'd assured them time and time again that within three years, he could guarantee them a twenty percent return on their investment, while simultaneously laundering their money for them.

The thick Eastern European accent on the other end of the call uttered only four words before the line went dead.

"You have three years."

Chapter Eleven

He arrived in a rental car around 4:00 pm, just as the sun began to slip behind the trees lining the mountain range to the west of Wilcox County. This was a departure from his usual preference for using UBER or Lyft, which allowed him to work on his notebook during the ride.

Maxwell wasn't particularly social when it came to other people. As a broker, he'd conditioned himself to keep his information and financial relationships close to the vest. Even after working with him for years, Katherine knew very little about him beyond the investment projects on which they'd collaborated.

Odin knew him. He'd been at the big party for Katherine and Roger by the lake last year, and his cologne told Odin he'd also been in Katherine's office that day... which seemed odd because none of the other guests from the party ever went into that room. There was something else, but Odin just couldn't remember.

In any case, Odin did not trust Maxwell at all. To Odin, he always seemed to be playing "guess which hand"; the game Roger and Odin played when Odin would find the hand Roger was hiding the treats in. With Maxwell, there was never a treat for anyone… just two empty hands, and today those hands were sweating.

Odin watched as Katherine met Maxwell at the screen door, and then walked inside with him. He followed after them quietly, letting the screen door catch on his tail to prevent it from slamming as it closed.

Without a sound, he crouched in the dark hallway just outside Katherine's office.

Inside the office, Katherine had already downloaded the files Maxwell had requested onto a thumb drive. As she sat down behind her desk, Maxwell sat in the chair across from her with his back to the door.

"You know, Max, I could easily have sent these to you using the company's encrypted server," Katherine said. "It would have saved you a lot of driving time."

Maxwell smiled, saying, "I love coming down here once in a while. It's always so peaceful here. No one around to bother you, and no nosey neighbors to deal with." Just then, Isabel came down the stairs, with her tablet in hand. She'd been upstairs doing her homework assignment and wanted Katherine to check her answers.

As usual, she walked right past Odin and into the office without knocking.

"Auntie Katie, can you see if I got everything right this time? I think…"

Isabel's voice trailed off into silence when she noticed Maxwell was in the room and had turned to look at her. All the color left her face, and she just stood there transfixed, as the tablet fell from her hands to the floor.

Maxwell stood up from the chair, saying, "Hi, Isabel."

As he took a step toward her, Katherine watched Isabel's eyes pool over with tears. The urine running down her leg formed a puddle on the floor between her feet.

"Maxwell, what did you do!?" Katherine screamed.

Odin already knew the answer to that question.

As Maxwell turned to look at Katherine, he said… "Loose ends. Just tying up loose ends."

"I don't understand," said Katherine.

"Of course, you don't! You didn't lose your ass in that real estate deal… I did!" screamed Maxwell. "Had you not abandoned the project, maybe the others would have stayed, but no! You left! Everyone left!"

"You said you got out clean," Katherine said. "You told me you got out clean!"

"I lied!" screamed Maxwell.

"But why?" asked Katherine, stalling… looking beyond the door at Odin in the hallway shadows.

"The money I used was dirty!" Maxwell said. "I thought it was a sure thing! You always deliver a sure thing!"

"Listen, Maxwell. We can talk about it. Roger will be back any minute now, and we can all…"

"No, he won't be back, Katherine," stated Maxwell flatly. "I'm the one who set up the trip he's on, and he won't be back until tomorrow night."

From the hallway, Odin was watching Katherine closely. He knew her distress gestures very well. With her right palm out angled slightly downward, she was telling him to wait… but be ready.

As Maxwell grabbed Isabel by the arm, snatching her abruptly towards the chair he'd been sitting in, Odin watched… but waited.

"Sit down!" he said to Isabel, pulling a revolver from his jacket pocket. Isabel was in shock, still staring at Maxwell as she slumped into the chair.

Chloe had been upstairs with Isabel, sleeping under her desk. When she heard Maxwell raising his voice, she immediately headed down the stairs, where she saw Odin in the shadows outside the office. Without a sound, she crept up behind him. Together, they sat silently in the darkness.

In that moment when Maxwell had turned to reach for Isabel, Katherine quickly tapped the LIVE STREAMING icon on her desktop PC. Although no conference was scheduled, anyone on the network would hear the video conference alert, and could join the live feed... If anyone even noticed.

Looking down at Isabel, Maxwell said, "You just had to pick this room to have your fucking tea party! You shouldn't have been spying on me."

Isabel often hid underneath Katherine's desk to play with her dolls. It was her not-so-secret hideout.

Maxwell had completely overlooked her at first, when he accessed Katherine's computer to install covert decryption software.

The software... had he been able to complete the setup and transmit the IP address to his smartphone... would have made it unnecessary for him to ever return. It would have allowed him to simply copy and manipulate any files, programs, or documents on her encrypted network, without her even knowing about it.

Unfortunately, Isabel revealed herself before he could link the mirroring software to his smartphone.

Although he wasn't sure whether she would do or say anything to arouse suspicion, he left the office, knowing he could return and recover the hidden files embedded in the program manually, once he'd gotten the information he needed.

He'd hung around for a few days, waiting for the opportunity to slip back into the house unnoticed to retrieve the decrypted information. He was absolutely stunned when Isabel recognized him at the park.

"I remember you!" Isabel said loudly, pointing her finger at him. "You were the man playing with Auntie Katie's computer!"

He was so shocked, that he instinctively lunged at her, with the sole intention of keeping her quiet. When she stepped backward to avoid him, she'd stumbled over the exposed root of a tree, falling hard and cracking the back of her head against a large rock on the ground.

She wasn't moving, and as far as he could tell, she wasn't breathing either.

Panicking, he snatched Isabel's arm, literally dragging her limp body up the hill behind the park. In the distance, he could see people running towards them, calling out her name.

Upon reaching the firebreak where he'd parked an old pickup truck, he tossed her body into the back like a sack of garbage. Before his pursuers on foot could reach him, he sped off, kicking up dust and gravel to obscure the vehicle license plates.

He'd planned to use the old dirt firebreak road to get close enough to Roger's and Katherine's house, so he could slip in and out on foot without being seen. He'd timed their evening walks many times and knew exactly how much time he had to extract the information from Katherine's computer. What he didn't need was a little girl's body to be discovered rolling around in the back of his truck.

Years earlier, in an attempt to perpetrate insurance fraud, he'd removed the tools and typical "theft" loot from a failed construction project and dumped it into a sinkhole he'd discovered deep in the woods. Later he went back and burnt the entire site to the ground. That sinkhole was where he dumped Isabel, believing she'd be swallowed up and forgotten, just like the other "junk" he'd disposed of there.

Never in a million years would he have imagined himself in the middle of this mess. What he did know was that without the files he came for, going to prison would be the least of his worries.

"Here's everything you asked for," said Katherine. "Just take it and go. There's no reason to hurt anyone."

"Katherine, I don't need that worthless shit! Do you really think I'd drive two and a half hours out to 'See-Y'all-Later-Land' for some ridiculous quarterly projections?

"Maybe I'll go take a dip in the crick, and have some sarsaparilla tea while I'm here!" chided Maxwell, using his most sarcastic Southern Belle accent.

Reaching into his pants pocket, he withdrew a thumb drive and handed it to Katherine. "Just plug it in, and when the prompt screen appears, hit enter," he said.

Katherine inserted the drive, and in the next second, three things happened… almost simultaneously.

Katherine hit ENTER, while closing her right hand into a fist. Odin saw Katherine's hand signal and exploded out of the dark hallway, leaping viciously toward Maxwell as he raised the revolver, pointed it at Katherine... and fired.

In the confines of Katherine's office, the sound of the gunshot was deafening. Isabel shrank even deeper into the office chair, clutching her hands over her ears as Odin sailed past her. The impact of Odin slamming into Maxwell's back knocked him from his feet into the heavy wooden desk separating him from Katherine as she slid to the floor, leaving a thick trail of blood down the already spattered wall.

Pinning him against the desk, Odin's sank his teeth deeply into Maxwell's right shoulder, rapidly shaking his head from side to side. Maxwell, frantically attempting to regain his balance, felt as if his right arm was being ripped from his body.

Isabel ran screaming from the office and back up the stairs to her room, with Chloe right behind her. She pressed herself into the corner behind the dresser, closing her eyes tightly and making herself as small as possible. Chloe backed up against Isabel, facing outward, and pressing the little girl even tighter into the corner. She would die before letting anyone past her.

In Katherine's office, Odin and Maxwell were on the floor locked in a deadly battle. Another shot rang out as Maxwell, unable to lift his arm and aim, fired wildly into the room, hoping to scare off the executioner ripping into his shoulder. Odin was unfazed by the sound of the gunfire, clamping down even tighter as he felt Maxwell's clavicle crumble under the immense pressure exerted by his powerful jaws.

Maxwell, pinned beneath the desk, screamed out in agony while attempting to free himself from the bloodstained floor. Using his left arm, he jabbed his elbow forcefully into Odin's ribs over and over again, attempting to dislodge him. He'd already lost a lot of blood, and was on the verge of losing consciousness.

Each time he tried pushing himself up, his hand would slip on the ever-slickening surface, under the weight and relentless shaking of Odin's enormous body.

Taking the revolver from his useless right hand into the left one, he fired wildly over his left shoulder.

Odin yelped loudly, finally releasing his death-grip on Maxwell, and falling to the floor on his side. The two of them lay there, facing one another, breathing heavily.

Suddenly, Odin was very tired. He thought he'd just lay there for a while and rest.

During the fight, he'd heard Isabel and Chloe run up the stairs to her room. He knew Chloe would protect Isabel from anything, and this guy on the floor next to him… he wasn't going anywhere.

Maxwell had lost a lot of blood. His right arm was a useless stump, dangling from his mutilated shoulder like some obscenely misshapen piñata. In his left hand, he still held the revolver. Lifting it slowly, he placed it against Odin's head, saying, "Good night, old boy."

Odin closed his eyes and thought to himself, *Katherine will come for me. She always comes for me.*

Maxwell never saw the bat crashing down across his face. Over, and over, and over again, Katherine swung that Louisville Slugger until there was nothing worthwhile left to swing at.

Outside, the distant sound of sirens echoed through the night, and flashing blue and red lights filtered through the house into the room. Katherine, bleeding badly from her left shoulder, sat on the floor beside Odin and lifted his giant head onto her lap. Leaning back against the wall, she whispered, "Good boy, Odin… Good, good, boy."

Odin was ever so tired.

As Katherine sat on the floor of her office, watching the red and blue lights dancing on the walls and ceiling, she inserted her right index finger into the bullet hole in her upper left chest. Her left index finger was plugging the hole in Odin's neck. They'd both lost a lot of blood, but honestly, it was difficult to tell how much, because half the floor in her office was covered in it.

Within a few seconds, which seemed like hours to Katherine, Sheriff Ward and two deputies entered the room with weapons drawn. They quickly assessed the situation, and realizing there was no longer an imminent threat, called for the paramedics who were already staged outside the front door. Holstering his sidearm, the Sheriff knelt beside Katherine asking, "Is there anyone else in the house?"

"Isabel is upstairs…" Katherine whispered.

Sheriff Ward nodded in their direction, and one of the deputies rushed up the stairs with the other following as back-up. Reaching Isabel's room, they opened the door to find Chloe backed into the corner next to the dresser. The fur along her back was hackled and she was growling viciously toward the two officers in the doorway. Behind her in the same corner, Isabel peeked cautiously over the edge of the dresser.

As the first deputy advanced toward Isabel, Chloe lunged forward, barking violently and forcing him to retreat. Then she receded into the corner, blocking any path to Isabel.

"You're gonna have to take that dog down!" shouted the back-up deputy.

"NO!" cried Isabel, squeezing past Chloe's rump and throwing her arms around her dog's neck. "It's okay, Chloe," she said. "They're good grownups."

After a few seconds, Chloe settled down but never took her eyes off of the two armed men.

When they approached again, weapons holstered, one deputy slowly reached towards Isabel. She cautiously took his hand, and walked toward him with Chloe in close tow. As they exited the room and made their way down the stairs, one of the deputies removed his jacket, placing it over Isabel's head, to prevent her from seeing the gruesome aftermath of the carnage which had transpired in Katherine's office.

At the front door, paramedics lifted Isabel onto a gurney, wheeling her toward one of the waiting ambulances. Chloe followed close behind, and watched as they loaded her in, closing the doors behind them.

When the engine started, Chloe's eyes and ears perked up, and as the ambulance began to move, so did Chloe.

Making its way through the numerous emergency vehicles in the driveway, the ambulance finally reached the main road, accelerating towards New Gatwick Bridge.

In fewer than five minutes, they were pulling into the Wilcox County Medical Center roundabout, and right up to the ER ramp. The driver exited the ambulance and walked quickly to the back to open the doors. His eyes widened in disbelief, then softened into a smile as he saw Chloe obediently sitting there, waiting for Isabel to emerge.

"Hey, isn't that…?"

"Chloe!" Isabel cried, upon seeing her best friend was already there. "I told them you'd be here!"

Turning to the ER nurse walking beside the gurney, Isabel asked, "Can Chloe come with me?"

"I'm sorry, sweetheart, but dogs aren't allowed in the emergency rooms," replied the nurse.

"How about I keep an eye on her while the doctors check you out?" asked the driver.

"Okay," said Isabel, visibly disappointed.

When they began pushing the gurney inside, Chloe began to follow.

"No, Chloe," Isabel said. "You have to stay with… What is your name, sir?"

"My name's Bishop," replied the driver.

"You stay with Bishop, Chloe," Isabel finished.

Chloe looked up at Bishop then back at Isabel, but remained seated beside him when they wheeled her through the ER doors. Inside, as they pushed Isabel down the long corridor, the nurse asked, "Did Chloe ride here with you?"

"No," replied Isabel.

"Well, how did she get here so fast?" asked the nurse, smiling.

"Odin taught her how to fly," said Isabel, without a single doubt in her mind.

Chapter Twelve

Roger had just checked in at the hotel when he received the teleconference notification from Katherine's computer. His Blackberry vibrated inside his jacket pocket while buzzing quietly on the elevator ride up to his floor. Katherine hadn't mentioned any scheduled virtual meetings or conferences over the weekend, so it was likely something that had come up while he was en route to San Diego.

After hanging his suits in the closet and placing his toiletries in the bathroom, Roger kicked off his shoes and stretched out across the bed. Whatever Katherine was streaming was getting quite a bit of attention.

Alerts for individuals joining the video conference were coming in every few seconds, and by the time Roger joined the feed, there were already 112 viewers.

His curiosity mounted as he watched the little blue buffering icon making its rounds. 10%, 20%, 45%, 60%, 80%, 97%, 100%, and finally "Rendering video." When the images appeared, the front and rear-facing video camera feeds appeared side-by-side in a split screen layout. The front-facing camera showed Katherine with her hands raised, and palms facing outward. The rear-facing camera clearly showed Isabel's horrified expression, with

Maxwell's left hand on her shoulder, and a revolver in his right hand pointed at Katherine!

Unable to believe his own eyes, Roger pushed and held the volume gain button until it reached maximum, just in time for the first shot to ring out! He watched in horror as Katherine fell back against the wall, leaving a trail of blood behind her as she slumped to the floor and out of the camera's field of view.

By that time, several viewers had indicated in comments to the live feed that they'd notified local law enforcement, and help was already on the way. Before Maxwell could turn his weapon on Isabel, Odin sailed into view, knocking him to the floor and completely out of sight. There were sounds of an intense struggle, and a fleeting view of Isabel and Chloe running out of the room towards the stairs.

Odin's ceaseless, low growl and Maxwell's screams of agony were bone-chilling proof that Odin was going to kill Maxwell... the man who'd dared to harm Katherine and Isabel.

Roger's body involuntarily recoiled as additional gunshots punctuated the sounds of the life and death struggle being waged in Katherine's office, and broadcast live around the world. One final gunshot rang out in the room, followed by Odin's loud yelp, and a long silence.

The tension was palpable with the clicking sound of a hammer being drawn back, and Maxwell's garbled voice muttering something unintelligible to those watching the live feed.

Suddenly, Katherine appeared out of nowhere. The entire left side of her blouse was soaked with blood as she swung the baseball bat Roger kept behind the front door, just in case. She continued to swing until the exertion and blood loss left her too weak to continue. The sound of the baseball bat falling to the floor signaled the end of the deadly confrontation.

Shortly thereafter, Sheriff Ward and his deputies stormed into the office, clearing it for emergency personnel to enter. Moments later, the live feed was cut, but by that time, Roger was already on his way back to the airport.

Katherine and Odin wouldn't be riding in the same ambulance this time. Both had suffered serious injuries which required immediate medical attention. Still, Katherine refused to remove her finger from Odin's wound, or let paramedics transport her anywhere until she knew Isabel was safe, and that help had also arrived for Odin.

It was less than a minute before Isabel and Chloe passed by the office door with the deputies, on their way to the paramedic team waiting in the living room.

The team preparing to transport Katherine was growing impatient, worried about the amount of blood she'd already lost. "We've got to move her right now!" said one of the paramedics, reaching out to remove her left hand from Odin's neck.

Katherine quickly grabbed the collar of his coat with her right hand and pulled his face to within an inch of hers. "If you even try to move my left hand," she said, "I will use this one here, to pick up that bat over there and beat your ass with it!" The look in her eyes could have melted a glacier as she asked, "Are we clear?"

At that moment, she felt another hand… a gentle one… placed atop hers and turned to find Odin's veterinarian there looking at her.

"I've got this, Mrs. O'Connor," said Dr. Forrester. "I'll take it from here."

Katherine nodded and closed her eyes… her hand falling away from Odin's neck, as she finally lost consciousness. The paramedics quickly whisked her out of the house and into the ambulance waiting outside.

Dr. Forrester and Odin were hot on their heels, departing the house less than two minutes later.

Medical teams at both the Wilcox County Medical Center, and the Wilcox County Animal Hospital were prepped and waiting for their respective charges to arrive. When they did, both teams went to work immediately to save the lives of their patients.

Katherine's injury would have been far less traumatic under most circumstances. The small .32 caliber bullet had entered her chest above and to the left of her heart, passing completely through her body, but fracturing and partially fragmenting against her left scapula. The bone and bullet fragments would have been much easier to remove had she been able to remain stationary until the paramedics arrived.

Unfortunately, that was not the case.

Katherine's adrenalin-assisted berserker rage with the baseball bat had caused the fragments to move, cutting into the muscle tissue, cartilage, and arteries in close proximity to her heart. The internal bleeding and tissue damage were far more extensive than they otherwise would have been. Removing those fragments and repairing the damage caused by them would require a lengthy and risky surgery.

Assessing the situation and injuries at hand, Katherine's surgical team settled in for a long night in the operating room.

Odin's situation could have and would have been much more serious had the projectile been larger, or entered from a slightly different angle, or had the point of entry been a bit higher or lower. Had any of those things varied by even the slightest of tolerances, Odin's death would have been immediate and unavoidable.

By whatever miracle had protected him that day, Odin had once again escaped near-certain death by the narrowest of circumstances.

As with Katherine, the bullet had passed completely through Odin's body; however, the entry and exit wounds were much cleaner. The bullet entered above the cluster of major blood vessels running along his neck and throat, traveling through and exiting below his spine. As it passed through, it grazed the underside of his spinal cord but did not sever it. The jolt caused by the projectile brushing against those raw nerves produced a temporary paralytic effect, similar to that of someone being shot by a Taser.

Katherine's finger inside the wound had also greatly stemmed Odin's blood loss, so within an hour after the start of his surgery, Dr. Forrester and the surgical team were confident Odin would recover swiftly and completely, and he was already in the recovery room when Roger's plane touched down at the airport.

As soon as he reached the gate, Roger made a beeline straight to Wilcox County Medical Center, where he'd been pacing back and forth in the waiting room for hours. Every time the door leading to that long empty corridor opened, he'd turn toward it, hoping for news or an update regarding Katherine's condition.

Barbara and David had arrived hours earlier to pick up Isabel and Chloe after Isabel had been examined and released with a clean bill of health. Despite the ordeal she'd just been through, she was emotionally in good spirits and happy to see her parents when they walked into the examination room where she'd been waiting.

David was signing Isabel's release documents when Roger arrived. Barbara walked up to him and, placing her arms around his neck, she hugged him tightly. Isabel also squeezed in and hugged him around his waist, and after signing the release paperwork, David joined them in the family huddle, as they all stood there in quiet disbelief.

Barbara broke the silence, saying, "Katherine is a fighter, Roger. She'll be back on her feet in no time, and we're all praying for her."

"It's all just so bizarre," stated Roger. "I was watching when he pulled the trigger and I still couldn't comprehend what I was seeing there. It was just so unbelievable."

Yet, there they all stood, dealing with the very vivid reality of Katherine fighting for her life a few yards from them, down that long dark hallway.

"Would you like for one of us to stay with you?" asked Barbara.

"No. You guys go on home. It's been a long day for everyone, and you guys deserve some family time. I will call you immediately if there's any news," said Roger.

As they left through the emergency room exit, Isabel turned back to smile and wave at Roger one more time before the sliding glass doors closed behind them.

Outside, Chloe was still waiting patiently with Bishop, even after hours of unwavering surveillance of the ER exit doors. Upon seeing Isabel walk out through them, Chloe bolted toward her, elated at the safe return of her very best friend. Isabel hugged her tightly, happily absorbing dozens of adoring licks and kisses before turning her attention to the ambulance driver.

"Thank you for watching out for her, Mr. Bishop. I hope she wasn't too much trouble for you."

"Trouble?" replied Bishop, chuckling. "She barely even moved while you were in there!"

Happy to have this stage of the ordeal behind them, Barbara and David loaded Isabel and Chloe into the back of their car. Before they even cleared the parking lot, Isabel was sound asleep with her arms wrapped tightly around Chloe's neck.

Earlier that evening, Dr. Forrester had also called Roger to check on Katherine, and to let him know Odin was out of surgery. She explained to him that Odin's surgery had gone well, and that he was expected to make a full recovery.

Roger asked Dr. Forrester if she wouldn't mind keeping Odin there until the next morning, so he could stay close to Katherine until she was out of surgery.

"Of course," replied Dr. Forrester. "I'd like to keep him overnight for observation anyway, just to be sure there are no unforeseen complications. He'll be in good hands here until you're ready to pick him up."

It was nearly 2:00 a.m. when the surgeon final emerged from the ER hallway. He appeared to be exhausted, but he did manage a smile when Roger approached him.

"Mr. O'Connor?" asked the surgeon extending his hand to Roger.

"Yes!" Roger said, shaking the doctor's hand.

"I'm Dr. Melbourne, your wife's surgeon, and I wanted to tell you personally that the surgery went very well."

Roger breathed an audible sigh of relief at the news.

"There was a lot of internal damage to both the bone and the soft tissue where the bullet struck her. When it entered, it glanced off of her shoulder blade and fragmented, with part of it passing through and exiting out of her back, and other parts ricocheting around inside her upper chest and shoulder area. Then, while she was defending herself, those tiny bullet fragments and bone splinters were spread even further throughout her upper left chest cavity. It took a while to collect all the debris and repair the damage," explained the doctor.

"We fixed the damaged blood vessels and stopped the bleeding, and we're pretty sure we got everything," said Dr. Melbourne. "Still…" he continued, "we'd like to keep her here, and sedated for a few days, just to be on the safe side."

Placing his hand on Roger's shoulder, Dr. Melbourne said, "She's been through a lot, Mr. O'Connor. She's going to need a lot of support while she recovers, and it will take some time. We'll do everything we can, but the rest will be up to her, and how hard she's willing to fight for a full recovery."

"Thank you, Dr. Melbourne," said Roger. "For everything."

As the doctor left the waiting room, walking back down the long, dark hallway beyond the double doors, Roger smiled to himself. Just a few hours ago, he'd seen this woman take a bullet, and then pummel her assailant with a baseball bat in order to protect her family.

If ever there was a fighter… it was Katherine.

Chapter Thirteen

Odin hadn't spent a night without Katherine near him since he was a puppy. When he awoke inside a cage in the recovery room of the animal hospital, he was completely disoriented. Dr. Forrester placed him in the cage to keep him from moving around too much, should he awaken during the night. She wanted to make sure he didn't re-injure himself, so the top of the cage was relatively low, making it far more comfortable for him to lie down than to stand up inside it.

When she came into the recovery room, Odin was patiently sitting there like the Sphinx, watching her through groggy eyes.

"Hi, Odin!" she said, surprised to see he was even awake. "How are you feeling today, big guy?"

Taking a seat on the floor in front of the cage, she opened it to let him out. He was still a bit wobbly from the anesthesia, but he did manage to stand and walk out of the cage under his own power.

The wound on Odin's neck was cleaned and dressed, then covered with a wide "BiteNot" collar to prevent him from scratching at, and reopening the sutures when he awoke. His legs were still a bit shaky, but he did manage to take a few more steps forward, laying his head on Dr. Forrester's shoulder. Patting his back and withers, she said, "Odin, you are one very special dog. I'm beginning to think you're invincible."

Just then, there was a knock at the door, and in stepped Roger holding a plastic bag. "Hey, Odin!" he said, taking a knee in front of him.

Odin was happy to see Roger, but it was obvious to everyone that he was really looking for Katherine.

"I know," said Roger. "You're looking for Mama, aren't you?"

Odin tilted his head to one side as if he were asking, "Where is she? Where is Mama?"

"Mama is at the 'people' hospital," said Roger. "They told me you can come and visit her when they move her into her own room this evening, but you've got to wear this…"

Reaching into the bag, Roger pulled out a blue vest with the words SERVICE DOG embroidered onto both sides, and a Velcro patch with Odin's name on it.

Looking at Dr. Forrester, Roger said, "Sheriff Ward told me you had something to do with this."

"He's more than earned it," she replied. "He's a hero." Together, they helped Odin into his new vest, and although he wasn't sure what it was, or why he had to wear it, if that's what it took for him to see Katherine, he was all for it.

After giving Roger detailed instructions on Odin's outpatient care over the next few days, the two of them left on their way to David and Barbara's house. Since their own house was still a crime scene, it would be a few days before the clean-up crew could sanitize everything, and they could return to their home. Barbara was at Wilcox County

Medical Center with her sister, but David, Isabel, and Chloe all greeted Roger and Odin at the car as they pulled up to the house. Odin was expecting to find Katherine on the front porch when they got there. When she wasn't, he searched the entire house with Isabel and Chloe behind him every step of the way.

While making their way back into the living room, Roger's phone rang. It was Barbara letting them know Katherine had been moved to a private room, and they could see her now.

Fifteen minutes later, Roger and Odin—decked out in his new SERVICE DOG vest—strode confidently past the reception desk, to the elevators that would take them to Katherine's room on the third floor. When they reached the room, Katherine was asleep.

Roger leaned over her, kissing her on the forehead while Odin softly licked her right hand. Surprisingly, Katherine was roused from her slumber just long enough to mutter… "Ah, my boys are here…" before falling back to sleep.

While Barbara and Roger were quietly talking to one another, Odin found a spot on the floor right beside Katherine's bed. After circling the spot three or four times, he curled himself into a giant black pillow.

Soon Barbara left the room, and Roger sat down on the recliner across from Katherine's bed.

Finally, thought Odin, *we're all together.*

Within minutes, they were all asleep.

Katherine remained in the hospital for several more days, and underwent two more surgeries to remove fragments that were missed during the initial operation. Although it was impossible to know if they'd missed anything else, Dr. Melbourne decided it was certainly more of a strain to her system to keep fishing around inside her chest, than it would be to simply allow her body to heal around any other fragments which may have eluded him.

Of course, he would carefully monitor her recovery and rehabilitation over the next few months but would only intervene surgically if it were absolutely necessary.

A few days later, Katherine was cleared to go home.

Chapter Fourteen

Even with the extent of her injuries, Katherine was determined to work at regaining her previous healthy and active lifestyle. She refused to let Maxwell take that from beyond the grave, after already having lost so much because of him.

The first few days at home were unexpectedly difficult for her. Even though the crime scene restoration crew had completely sanitized and repainted her office, the psychological scars from having been attacked and nearly killed in her own home were deeper than she anticipated.

She couldn't shake the image of him raising that gun and actually firing at her, or the sounds of Odin struggling with him as she dragged herself out into the hallway. An aluminum baseball bat behind the door had replaced the wooden one, but the memories it invoked were nonetheless haunting.

During the rehabilitation process, Odin and Roger were her twin pillars of strength, doing everything possible to make life's everyday tasks manageable for her. Roger took care of all the housework, and even turned out to be quite the cook! Odin was Katherine's constant shadow. He was literally never more than three steps away from her.

During her home rehabilitation sessions, Katherine's physical therapist, Louise, would put her through several different modalities designed to keep her from losing mobility while improving her overall range of motion. Louise couldn't help but notice how carefully Odin would observe everything she did. From the color of the dumbbells, to the size of the latex bands she used for resistance training, nothing escaped his watchful eye.

He would sit directly behind her as if to examine all the exercises from the therapist's perspective, and seemed able to anticipate which exercise would come next. It dawned on her, Odin was learning her entire therapy routine. A few weeks into her rehabilitation sessions, she decided to test her theory.

After a few stretching and mobility exercises, without even looking at him, she said, "Odin, can you hand me one of those pink dumbbells?" When she turned around to see if he'd even understood her, she saw that the blue dumbbell was already on the floor right behind her, and Odin was sitting there, eyes and ears perked, waiting for her next request.

"Not the blue one," she said, smiling. "I need the pink one."

"No…" Katherine interjected. "Remember? We increased the weight to the blue ones last week."

Checking her tablet, she realized Katherine AND Odin were correct! She had increased the weight! "You are an amazing fella," said Louise, stroking Odin's head.

After that, she began incorporating Odin into all of Katherine's therapy sessions. She had to change a few of the modalities slightly, but for the most part, Odin was capable of assisting Katherine with all of her exercises... even without Louise's help.

By late spring, Katherine, Roger, and Odin had resumed their daily walks down to the old Gatwick Bridge.

Sometimes Isabel and Chloe would join them, but unlike before, Odin never let Katherine out of his sight. Even when darting ahead with Chloe to chase rabbits and squirrels, he was always mindful of her exact location.

Katherine and Odin continued the exercise regimen Louise had created for them, even after the twelve months covered by her health insurance benefit had been exhausted. Katherine was getting stronger, but somehow, she wasn't getting better, and Odin knew it.

Over two years after her surgeries, Katherine still didn't feel as if she'd fully left the episode behind her, or even regained the level of health she'd enjoyed prior to being shot. She exercised every day in spite of the persistent pain in her joints, yet after a certain point, she plateaued, and no matter what she did or how hard she worked to push past it, her efforts were futile.

Were it not for Roger and Odin, she wouldn't even have been able to function. She would often forget the simplest of things. Where did she leave her keys? What day of the week was it? Why did she come into the kitchen, and what was she looking for, standing there in front of the refrigerator with the doors wide open?

Added to that, she became increasingly irritated by the most mundane of things. Why was the television so loud? Who left the drinking glass on the counter instead of putting it directly into the dishwasher? Who forgot to replace the empty roll of toilet paper?

Once, she even yelled at Odin, saying… "You're always under foot! Are you trying to trip me on purpose!?"

Odin, while always very close to her, would never have allowed her to trip over him. He was far too alert, and far too observant of her, to ever let that happen.

In fact, most of the things that irritated her were actually things she'd done, but couldn't recall doing.

She'd leave things in places Odin knew weren't where they belonged, so he'd simply put them in their rightful places. She'd leave the refrigerator door open after going into the living room to watch television, and Odin would close it behind her without so much as a peep. Odin constantly scanned the floor for objects over which Katherine might accidentally trip and fall, and even when she yelled at him, he would never wander far from her side.

In spite of the delicious meals Roger prepared for them every single day, Katherine's appetite for food was fading and she was struggling to maintain a healthy weight. On those occasions when she did eat, within hours, and often within minutes, she'd become nauseous, throwing everything up again.

Roger would only use organic non-GMO foods and ingredients when preparing their meals, and he was meticulous in his research of foods which would boost her faltering immune system. For all sakes and purposes, Katherine's diet was amazingly healthy and very well balanced. Still, she was withering away right before their very eyes.

She tried to rationalize her symptoms away by claiming they were either coincidental, or just a normal part of getting older. According to Katherine, memory loss happens to everyone over fifty, and her nausea was simply caused by a passing stomach flu. Her dizzy spells were probably due to her new glasses, which were stronger than her old prescription lenses.

In winter, she coughed because of the cold. In spring, it was due to the pollen, and in the summer, it was either hay fever or high ozone levels.

Not every day was a bad one though. In spite of everything, Katherine still enjoyed her evening walks with Roger and Odin, even though they weren't as long as they had been in the past.

Returning from one of their evening outings, they were met by Barbara, David, and Isabel in their mini-van on the lane leading down to the driveway. When they parked, Isabel literally sprang from the back seat, running up to them.

"Uncle Roger... Aunty Katie..." she said excitedly, taking each of them by the hand. "We have a surprise for you!"

As they walked around to the back of the vehicle, David used the key remote to open the rear hatch. Chloe was inside, sitting dutifully next to a large wicker basket covered by a blanket. When Isabel moved the blanket aside, there were eight healthy little pups squirming around in the bottom of the basket.

"Oh my God!" exclaimed Katherine. "They are beautiful!"

Odin was pacing and bobbing in place, anxious to see what they were all looking at. Roger and Katherine each took a handle of the basket and placed it on the ground, so Odin could also see. Chloe hopped out of the back as well, and they both peered into the basket at what was obviously their own handiwork.

Odin took off like a shot, dashing around the yard as if he'd been shocked by a live wire! He would run out to the tree, then cut and run back to the basket and Chloe, then bolt off again. He'd run up to Roger and Katherine with his tongue hanging out, panting and tail wagging, then dart back to the basket and Chloe again.

After several minutes of this, he'd worn himself out, and laid down on his back next to the basket, still squirming around like he'd do when he wanted Katherine to rub his belly.

The most amazing thing of all... When he looked up at Katherine, she was laughing! For Odin, that was indeed a beautiful day.

Chapter Fifteen

Looking at all of those tiny little puppies squirming around in the basket brought tears to Katherine's eyes, but they were the happy kind. Odin was only a few days older than them the first time she held him, and it was difficult for her to imagine such tiny little babies growing into something of his size.

"They were just born last week!" said Isabel excitedly. "Dr. Forrester says they're all healthy, and Chloe is fine too!"

It dawned on Katherine that it had been weeks since she'd last seen Isabel and Chloe. In fact, other than Roger and Odin, she hadn't seen or spoken to anyone since… She couldn't even remember anymore.

"Linda at the shelter says she will help us get them all adopted after they're nine weeks old," Isabel said.

Katherine remembered Linda very well, clearly recalling their first encounter… as well as their second encounter on the same day.

Chapter Two (Revisited)

Linda had watched Katherine as she literally ran out the door of the clinic that day. Odin was squirming around in his blanket like crazy, and he wanted no part of her whatsoever. Rather than going back to the shelter, she decided to wait there in the clinic for a little while.

"Is there something wrong?" asked Dr. Forrester.

"She'll be back. I'm sure of it," said Linda.

Doctor Forrester was intrigued. "And what makes you so sure about that?"

"Did you not see the two of them together?" asked Linda. "He was like a natural part of her body when she held him, and he didn't even make a sound. He hasn't stopped squirming and whining since the second she handed him over to me."

"All pups are squirmy, Linda..." countered Dr. Forrester.

"Jen, that woman jumped into a freezing cold river this morning to pull him and the rest of his litter out of it. Then, she sat by the fireplace trying to save them all, and this little guy is the only one who made it."

"True, but..." Dr. Forrester started.

"I'm not finished..." interrupted Linda. "She then swaddled him in this very blanket and carried him pressed against her bosom, while she warmed the milk which she then fed to him through an eyedropper!

"Besides," Linda stated. "Her car is still in the parking lot."

Dr. Forrester turned to look out the door, just as Katherine was walking back in through it. Without hesitation, Linda walked over to Katherine and handed Odin back to her. He was asleep within seconds.

"Cow's milk is too rich for him," Linda said. "You're going to need some bitch milk, and you're going to need a lot of it. This milk contains all the proper nutrients to keep him healthy, until you can wean him onto solid food."

Katherine nodded, accepting the milk and asking, "How often and how much do I feed him?"

"Feed him whenever he's hungry," Linda said. "You'll know he's full when he falls asleep."

"How will I know when he's hungry?" asked Katherine.

"He'll be doing the exact opposite of what he's doing right now," replied Linda, nodding toward Odin.

"Puppies this young only do two things… eat and sleep. When he wakes up, feed him until he falls asleep again."

"That sounds like something even I can manage," said Katherine.

"It may take a few days for you to develop and synchronize your rhythms but trust me… you'll be fine," said Dr. Forrester. "You'll both be fine."

"If you need anything… anything at all, just call or come by," Linda added. "We're here for you."

As Katherine and Odin were about to leave the clinic, she stopped. Turning toward Linda, she asked, "How did you know I'd be back for him?"

"Well, Dr. Forrester told me you'd already named him," answered Linda. "When I saw the way you held him and the look on your face when you handed him over to me… I knew you loved him, and that I wouldn't be holding him for very long. I was surprised you actually made it out the door."

"I love him, huh?" Katherine said, smiling down at Odin.

"Well, I guess love at first sight, really does exist…"

Chapter Fifteen (Resumed)

Looking down at all those fur babies with Odin and Chloe sitting there, proudly watching over them, Katherine was oddly at peace.

"I want you to have one of them, Aunty Katie," said Isabel. "You can choose whichever one you want."

"How on earth could I ever choose? They're all so beautiful," said Katherine.

"Well," said Isabel, reaching into the basket and picking up one of the pups, "this one looks just like Odin."

Taking the pup from Isabel, Katherine said, "Oh my goodness. He does look like Odin!"

Holding him out in front of her, Katherine compared the pup to Odin, who sat there watching, approvingly. Save for Odin's ever-whitening whiskers and enormous size, there was definitely an unmistakable resemblance between the two of them.

"He's perfect, Isabel! Thank you!" said Katherine, placing the pup back into the basket with his brothers and sisters.

David and Roger carefully lifted the basket back into the van, and Chloe jumped in to take her place beside it as the rear hatch closed. Katherine hugged Barbara and David, then bent down to hug Isabel before watching them get back into the mini-van.

"Thank you for bringing them by for us to see," Said Katherine, as David backed up, then headed out the driveway towards the lane. Roger stood next to Katherine in the front yard with his arm around her shoulders, and Odin sat in the grass next to them as they waved at the van disappearing over the hill.

It was the last time Katherine would ever see Chloe and the pups again.

Chapter Sixteen

It was late summer in Wilcox County, and the leaves adorning the mountains had already begun to change.

The dark green foliage of the pines and red cedars was beautifully interspersed with the bright reds and yellows of the turning sugar maples and green ash.

Every morning, Katherine would sit on the front porch with Odin to enjoy her first cup of coffee and admire the beauty of the surrounding landscape, as the sunrise slowly burnt off the morning fog.

It had been only a few weeks since Barbara, David, and Isabel had come over to celebrate the Labor Day weekend with them. At that time, autumn and its cooler temperatures seemed an eternity away. Now, it was all but knocking on the door.

Roger was already in the kitchen making breakfast for them. It had been so long since she'd enjoyed a real country breakfast, and the smell of bacon, scrambled eggs, and hot biscuits was just what she'd been craving.

As she sat there sipping her coffee with one hand and scratching Odin's head with the other, her right hand began to tremble. She tried to put the cup down on the table beside her, but unable to control her hand, it fell to the floor instead, shattering.

Odin bolted upright and began barking to alert Roger, who rushed out to the porch immediately. By then, Katherine was in full seizure, and her whole body was shaking uncontrollably.

Roger dialed 9 1 1 and requested an ambulance immediately, then rolled her onto her left side and held her there to make sure her airway remained clear.

Within minutes, Odin saw the ambulance at the hilltop, and rushed up the lane to meet it. Barking non-stop, he escorted the paramedics back to the house and up to the porch where Katherine was lying in Roger's arms.

They immediately went to work, stabilizing her for transport to WCMC. While they loaded her into the ambulance, Roger ran into the house to grab his keys, and Odin's service dog vest. Then, jumping into his truck, he and Odin followed the ambulance right up to the emergency room entrance, where the paramedics wheeled her in.

"This is as far as you two can go," said the emergency room attendant. "We'll do everything we can to take care of her, but you two will have to stay in the waiting room while we do."

Roger nodded, and looking down at Odin said, "Come on, boy. We need to make some calls." Taking a seat in the waiting room near the ER corridor, Roger called Barbara and David, as well as Katherine's parents, while Odin sat on the floor beside him, unflinching, watching the double doors separating them from Katherine.

Barbara, David, and Isabel arrived in the waiting room just a few minutes before Katherine's parents did. As they spoke to, and comforted one another, Odin's eyes never left the double doors. Suddenly, he stood up and walked over to them. Everyone stopped and turned towards Odin, just as the ER doctor came out into the waiting room.

Approaching Roger, the doctor said, "I'm very sorry, Mr. O'Connor. We did everything we could, but she suffered catastrophic organ failure on the way here."

Roger was visibly stunned! "Organ failure? How can that be possible?" he asked

"It's hard to say without a thorough autopsy, but it looks like she was poisoned," said the doctor.

For the past three years, Roger had prepared nearly every meal she'd eaten. If she'd ingested poison in any form, he'd have known it because they both ate the exact same food, prepared fresh by him every day; yet, he showed no signs of being poisoned.

"Can we see her?" asked Roger, fighting back the tears welling up in his eyes.

"I'll have the nurses clean her up and prepare a viewing room for you," said the doctor, then adding, "I'm very sorry for your loss."

Odin watched as the doctor turned and walked back through the doors and down the long hallway. Looking up at Roger, he could feel something was very wrong. Where was Katherine?

As the rest of the family gathered around Roger receiving the news of Katherine's passing, the weight of their sorrow was crushing. Odin sat quietly, watching, unsure of what was going on. A few minutes later, one of the nurses came in to escort them to the viewing room.

As he'd always done when visiting Katherine in the hospital, Odin laid on the floor beneath the head of her bed. The nurse explained to everyone that they had only one hour to visit with Katherine before she'd be moved to autopsy. After everyone else had gone, Roger and Odin remained in the room with her until the nurse returned.

"I'm very sorry for your loss, Mr. O'Connor," said the nurse. "We need to take her down to autopsy now."

Before leaving the room, Roger leaned over and kissed her forehead one last time. His eyes were red and swollen as he whispered, "I love you, Katherine."

Odin put his paws on the bed and stood next to her on his hind legs. He sniffed her whole body through the sheet before finally licking her hand goodbye. As they left the room, Odin knew Katherine was no longer there. Her body was, but Katherine was not. Together, Roger and Odin walked back up the long hallway to the waiting room where everyone was still gathered.

The nurse asked Roger to sign a release authorizing an autopsy to determine the cause of death. Even though by law, in cases of suspected foul play or death by other than natural causes, consent from the next of kin is not required, Roger also wanted to know what had happened to her. Giving his consent would allow the autopsy to proceed much faster than waiting for a legal mandate compelling one.

After signing the release document, Roger and Odin rejoined the rest of the family.

"Would you like for one of us to drive you two home?" asked Barbara.

"No…" Roger said. "You guys have your own sorrow and mourning to deal with. Odin and I will be fine, and we'll call you the moment we hear anything new."

They all left the ER waiting room together before parting and going their separate ways. In the parking lot, Roger opened the passenger side door for Odin.

After a moment, Odin jumped into the back of the pickup, where he'd always ridden, unable to take the spot next to Roger.

That was Katherine's spot, and Odin needed to make sure there was room for her, in case she wanted to ride home with them.

Chapter Seventeen

Cause of death: Homicide.

In the Medical Examiner's office, Roger sat in total shock at the sheer incredulity of the autopsy report he was holding. Earlier that morning, the Coroner's office had called Roger, informing him that the autopsy report was available; however, never in a thousand years would he have suspected these findings.

Looking up at the Medical Examiner, Roger asked, "Lead poisoning? How is that even possible?"

Guiding Roger through the lengthy report, he attempted to explain the unexplainable saying, "When Katherine was shot nearly three years ago, her surgeon literally spent hours, during three separate surgeries, removing bullet and bone fragments from her shoulder and chest cavity, and repairing the damage done to the nerves and blood vessels there."

"Yes," said Roger. "I remember."

"Unfortunately, in isolating and removing all of the debris, they missed something," the Medical Examiner explained. "A large piece of the lead projectile penetrated and remained lodged in the bone marrow of her scapula."

Roger sat there silently, trying to comprehend what he was hearing.

The M.E. continued, "Although her body healed around the fragment, it has been introducing lead directly into her circulatory system for years now, slowly poisoning her over time."

"How could that have been missed?" asked Roger.

The M.E. explained, "The symptoms are easily overlooked. Indications such as nausea and body aches are often written off as influenza, while persistent coughing might be attributed to a chest cold or allergies. Unless you connect all of the symptoms, or live in a city like Flint, Michigan, you might never even suspect lead poisoning."

"Are there any other symptoms?" asked Roger.

"Well," said the M.E., "there's increased irritability, short term memory loss, mood swings, dizziness, and balance issues…"

Listening to the list of symptoms, tears rolled down Roger's face as he realized Katherine had displayed nearly all of them… and he'd missed it. Although he'd taken her to the clinic to address many of the symptoms individually, he'd never put them all together.

"I should have done more research, or even made her undergo more thorough examinations…" Roger started.

"You cannot blame yourself for this, Mr. O'Connor," The M.E. interjected. "Most of the time, lead poisoning is determined by systematically eliminating the origin of each symptom. Unless you work in a high-risk job, or live in a high-risk environment, there's very little reason to suspect lead poisoning. Even competent healthcare professionals have misdiagnosed cases like this."

None of this made losing Katherine any less painful, nor did it lessen Roger's sense of guilt for failing her.

"Mr. O'Connor, Katherine was murdered," said the Medical Examiner, "and her assailant killed her nearly three years ago, with a fatal gunshot wound to the chest. Without your love and support, she wouldn't have even survived this long."

Roger silently nodded, fearing his voice would break if he attempted to speak. As he rose from his chair to leave, the Medical Examiner stood and walked over to him.

"You're a good man, Mr. O'Connor. Katherine was very fortunate to have had such a devoted husband, and I'm sure, she knew that."

His heart still heavy with grief, Roger left the Coroner's office with the autopsy report clutched tightly in his hand. After sharing the autopsy results with the rest of the family, Roger was emotionally drained. He hadn't slept in two days, and his whole world seemed to be off balance. The silence in the house was deafening, as his thoughts kept circling the events of the past few years, wondering what he could have done differently, if anything at all.

Looking out the front screen door, Roger saw Odin lying beside Katherine's chair on the front porch. He'd been nearly invisible for the past few days, either lying on the floor of Katherine's office, or there on the front porch waiting for her. His food bowl had remained untouched, since Katherine last fed him two days ago.

Honestly, neither of them had much of an appetite lately. Although several of their friends and neighbors had stopped by to express their condolences, all of them bringing enough food to feed a small army, most of it remained in the refrigerator… untouched.

Grabbing his jacket from the coat rack and heading out the front door, Roger said, "Come on, Odin. Let's take a walk."

Odin sprang to his feet and headed down the stairs behind Roger. In the yard, he paused for a moment to look back at the front door.

"It's just us today," Roger said.

Hesitating only a moment longer, Odin seemed to understand, finally turning toward Roger and trotting past him to lead the way up the lane. It wasn't at all unusual for Roger and Odin to go walking without Katherine. The unusual part would be going home to find she wasn't there anymore, but that was a thought for later. For now, it was just about the two of them getting out of the house and putting some distance between themselves and the tragedy of losing her.

It had been awhile since Odin was able to stretch out and run, just for the sake of running. He extended his gait, gaining speed as he passed the rusty skeleton of the old Gatwick Bridge.

Roger watched as Odin put more and more distance between them. "You go, boy," said Roger more to himself than to Odin who was well beyond earshot by now.

Odin stuck to the gravel walking path which ran parallel to the highway alongside Willis Creek for miles. By the time he passed the New Gatwick Bridge, he was in full stride, remembering how wonderful it felt to run so fast.

Settling on a spot atop a small rise where he could clearly see the entire section of the path between the two

Gatwicks, Odin enjoyed the warmth of the sun as he waited for Roger to come into view.

He'd waited here, watching Katherine and Roger many, many times, during their countless walks over the years.

They were always so happy together, and Odin missed Roger's happiness. He spotted Roger just as he was passing beneath the old bridge. Suddenly, Odin had an idea, and remembered something which might cheer Roger up a bit.

Like a thoroughbred horse leaving the gates, he bolted toward Roger approaching along the walking path.

Navigating his way down to the creek bed, Odin discovered exactly what he'd been searching for.

Appearing on the walking path, seemingly out of nowhere, Roger noticed Odin standing there. In his mouth, he was holding the perfect throwing stick. It was slightly waterlogged, but not too heavy to get some good distance on a throw. Odin trotted up to him, dropping the stick at Roger's feet.

For a moment, the two of them just stood there, looking at each other. Odin lowered his head with his tail in the air wagging excitedly as Roger reached down to pick up the smooth, damp stick. Leaning back like a pitcher winding up for the pitch, Roger threw the stick with all his might, sending it far upstream, splashing into the water.

Odin, running like the wind, leapt into the air, sailing far out into the waters of the widening Willis Creek.

Easily intercepting the stick in the water, Odin grabbed it, swimming back to the gravelly creek bank.

Running back up to the walking path, he dropped the stick directly at Roger's feet.

In spite of everything, Roger had to smile! Picking up the stick, he threw it again, this time even further upstream. Odin's athletic leaps and mid-air acrobatics were a sight to behold, each time resulting in him finding the stick and returning it to Roger for another throw.

Roger felt as if the weight of his emotional burden was being lifted with each subsequent throw of this perfect, soggy stick. By the time the sun began to slip behind the tree line, both of them were worn to a frazzle as they made their way back down the lane towards home. When they finally arrived back at the house, Roger sat down at the top of the porch steps, exhausted, as Odin laid down beside him, resting his head on Roger's lap.

They remained on the porch until well after dark, watching late season fireflies blinking in the night, and remembering the amazing times they'd shared with the love of BOTH their lives. Then, together, they went inside, ate dinner, and slept peacefully through the night.

Chapter Eighteen

Katherine's funeral was a small affair with only her parents, Barbara, David, Isabel, a few distant relatives, and a few close friends attending. She was interred next to her grandmother in the family cemetery on a hillside overlooking the Ocmulgee River basin.

Odin had visited the cemetery often with Katherine, when she'd cut fresh flowers to lay on her grandparents' graves. He'd never really understood the significance of that, but he always loved being there with her.

From here with his back to the forest, he could see their entire property, from the long narrow driveway leading down to the house, to the place where Willis Creek merged with the river, and beyond. It was one of his favorite places in the whole world.

As the interment ceremony drew to a close, Katherine's casket was lowered into the ground. Odin sat watchfully as Roger, Barbara, and Katherine's parents dropped flowers into the grave before leaving the ceremony with David and Isabel.

Odin remained behind as everyone else solemnly left the cemetery save for the two men covering Katherine's grave with earth. It reminded him of how he would bury special things he didn't want anyone else to find, so he could go back and enjoy them when no one else was around.

It didn't take long for the men to finish covering the grave. After loading their equipment and all the folding chairs onto a trailer, they left, driving back to the main road along the edge of the forest, rather than using the driveway, which was still filled with parked cars and trucks.

For the rest of the afternoon, people would come and go… some leaving after only a few minutes, and others remaining longer. Barbara, David, and Isabel were the last to depart, leaving the driveway empty, except for Roger's truck. Waving goodbye to them from the porch, Roger went into the house for a few minutes, then came back outside, wearing jeans and a flannel shirt.

Odin watched as he walked back up the hill toward the cemetery, then took a seat in the grass beside him. Odin lifted his head and placed it on Roger's lap.

Looking at each other as they sighed simultaneously, Roger asked Odin, "So, what's next, big boy?"

For the moment, Odin was satisfied just sitting there with Roger, looking out over the river. It had been a very long day, filled with people and emotions which were exhausting for both of them. They were relieved to finally have today's episode behind them, and as the sun began to set, Roger and Odin finally stood up, making their way back down the hill towards the house.

Suddenly, a car turned into the driveway at the top of the hill, driving slowly down toward the house. Odin recognized them before Roger did, and trotted ahead to meet them as they stopped near the porch.

Dr. Forrester and Linda got out of the car, waving at Roger, and bending down to pet Odin's enormous head.

"Hi, Mr. O'Connor," said Dr. Forrester, taking Roger's hand. "First, let me say how sorry we are for your loss. Katherine was an amazing woman, and we are all going to miss her very much."

"Thank you… Thank both of you," said Roger.

"We wanted to wait until everyone was gone, and you guys had some time to relax," said Linda, walking back towards the car, opening the back door. Reaching inside, she re-emerged, holding an excited little puppy in her hands! "Isabel told me this little guy belongs to you two."

Kneeling in front of Odin, Linda allowed him to say hello to the pup, who he recognized immediately! She then stood, handing the puppy to Roger, who was smiling from ear to ear.

"We also have some things you'll need to get him started off on the right foot," said Dr. Forrester, pulling a bag of food, a little bed, a pack of potty pads, and a bag of chew-toys out of the trunk of the car.

"Wow!" said Roger, reaching for his wallet.

"No, no," said Linda. "This is all yours at no charge to you."

"And, we'll waive the charges for all of his basic veterinary care for life," added Dr. Forrester. "Yours, too," she said, kneeling to pet Odin.

"What?" asked Roger, perplexed. "I… I don't get it."

Linda explained, "Barbara and Isabel wanted us to find good homes for all of Odin's and Chloe's puppies. She kept a girl and reserved this little guy for you. The rest of them, she wanted us to put up for adoption, with all the proceeds going to our charitable foundation in Katherine O'Connor's name."

Dr. Forrester jumped in. "Once the word got out who'd sired the pups, we got well over a thousand inquiries, wanting to reserve one of them... ANY one of them, for after they were weaned and ready for adoption."

"And that was only the first week!" added Linda.

"There were so many inquiries, that we couldn't keep up with them all, so we thought the only fair way to decide who'd get one was to sell raffle tickets."

"The raffle tickets were $25.00 each, which would include all adoption fees, scheduled wellness exams, and vaccinations for the entire first year," said Dr. Forrester.

"Really..." said Roger. "How many raffle tickets did you sell?"

"We sold over 8,000 of them!" exclaimed Linda.

"Katherine's donation to our Animal Clinic and Shelter was over two hundred thousand dollars!"

"Katherine will forever be our hero," said Dr. Forrester.

"Because of her and Odin here... we can almost guarantee Wilcox County will never have to put down another animal, just because it was lost or abandoned by its owner."

As they turned to walk back to the car, Linda said, "We ARE very sorry for your loss, Mr. O'Connor... She was our loss too."

After watching their tail lights disappear over the rise at the end of the driveway, Roger and Odin took the newest member of their family inside.

"Welcome home, little guy," said Roger, placing the puppy in the bed Odin had carried inside and placed on the floor next to his spot by the hearth. "It looks like Odin's already got a spot picked out for you."

Just like that, Odin was a guardian again.

Chapter Nineteen

Odin was fascinated by the puppy, even though he spent most of the day sleeping. When he did wake up, it was always to the sight of Odin looming over him... Not in a threatening way, but more like a drill sergeant trying to whip a new recruit into shape.

Odin showed him everything, and the puppy followed him around like a second shadow. He was clumsy and inattentive, and would fall asleep in the middle of... anything... including eating! Still, for Odin, every day with the puppy was like Christmas for him.

Eventually, Roger was able to settle on a new name for the pup. Since Katherine was born in the month of July, her birthstone, Onyx, became the pup's new name. He took to it right away, ignoring it at every opportunity!

The only time he really paid attention was when Odin was teaching him things, or when sticks and tennis balls were involved. He was seven months old when he discovered he loved water, and after that, it was impossible to keep him out of it. He and Odin were out and about daily, exploring either the forest along the property line, or the pebbled shores along the banks of Willis Creek.

True to their words, Dr. Forrester and Linda made sure both dogs remained healthy and happy as Onyx grew larger, and Odin grew older. Their evening walks with Roger continued, but now it was Onyx who ran ahead, clearing the path of rabbits and squirrels, and looking for those perfectly soggy sticks Roger would launch into the river for him to retrieve.

Occasionally, Isabel and Andrew would come by with Chloe and Onyx's sister, Penny. Odin and Chloe would sit on the porch watching the two younger dogs play with the same fervor and energy they themselves had once displayed, while Isabel and Andrew would sit together in the shade beneath the old oak tree in the front yard.

As it turned out, Andrew was indeed a very nice boy once his stepdad and Colin lost their influence over him. At the age of fourteen, he was already a handsome, strapping young man, taller than nearly everyone else in their class. When they were together, no one dared tease Isabel… and they were ALWAYS together.

Channeling his energy into football, Andrew became the quarterback and team captain, with Isabel watching and cheering him on from the sidelines during every single game. They were always laughing and giggling, and it was easy to see their bond was a deep and lasting one.

As Odin passed his knowledge on to Onyx, eventually he found himself falling behind. Onyx's stride lengthened and became stronger, while Odin's energy began to wane after nearly sixteen years of watching over their little piece of paradise, tucked away in Wilcox County.

Through it all, Odin never stopped missing Katherine, and each afternoon he would make the trek up the hillside to visit her, napping in the grass next to her grave, remembering her voice and how she'd call out for him when she couldn't find him.

He, of course, always knew where Katherine was, and would come immediately the moment she called his name.

Roger also knew Odin would disappear there to bathe in the sun and fall asleep in his favorite spot. If he couldn't be found anywhere else, Roger could always find him there.

It was a warm summer night in late August when Odin, feeling restless, walked quietly through the back door out into the moonlit backyard. His nose twitching, taking in the rich smells of the wooded river basin, he could sense a tightening in his chest, and it was difficult for him to breathe.

Looking into the distance, he made his way up the grassy hillside overlooking the river and the house below. By the time he reached his favorite spot in the whole world, his legs were shaking, and he was physically spent. Unable to go even a single step further, he laid down on his side, staring at her headstone across from him. When his vision began to fade, he thought to himself, *Katherine will come for me... She always comes for me.*

As he closed his eyes... she did, softly whispering to him. "Come on, big boy. It's time to go."

Odin opened his eyes to find Katherine standing there, right across from him! She was healthy and beautiful, and Odin was overjoyed at the sight of her.

Instinctively, he sprang to his feet, as she knelt beside him, wrapping her arms around his neck, as she'd done so many times before.

The tightness in his chest and the stiffness in his joints were gone, and Odin felt as if he could run forever.

Standing beside him, Katherine reached down and placed her hand atop Odin's head. Together, they flew up into and beyond a night sky, littered with stars as perfect as diamonds... none of which shone brighter than the two of them.

"Good boy, Odin... Good, good boy."

The End.